THE
DOCTOR'S
MISTRESS

BOOKS BY DANIEL HURST

THE DOCTOR'S WIFE SERIES

The Doctor's Wife

The Doctor's Widow

The Holiday Home

The Couple in the Cabin

The Intruder

What My Family Saw

The Accident

We Tell No One

The Couple at Table Six

We Used to Live Here

The Wrong Woman

He Was a Liar

The Woman at the Door

The Passenger

Til Death Do Us Part

THE
DOCTOR'S
MISTRESS

DANIEL HURST

bookouture

Published by Bookouture in 2023

An imprint of Storyfire Ltd.
Carmelite House
50 Victoria Embankment
London EC4Y 0DZ

www.bookouture.com

ISBN: 978-1-83525-088-4
eBook ISBN: 978-1-83525-087-7

PROLOGUE

The woman's piercing scream cuts through the air and makes everybody on the promenade stop what they are doing and turn to look. A panicking female with a pained expression on her face and tears sliding down her face is rushing along the seafront. And, just like that, her cries of 'Where is my baby?' shatter a beautiful day on the southwest coast of England.

This place is usually quiet, tranquil and beautiful. It's what this part of the world is known for. Cornwall, a popular tourist destination at any time of the year, is used to accommodating people who come for the views of the sandy beaches, the rugged cliffs and the quaint coves and villages. These same people also come for the ice cream, the fish and chips, the glass of beer or wine, and all of that comes with a spectacular sea view. Today has been no different, as hundreds of tourists stroll along the promenade and soak up the sun while deciding what they will do next in this pretty part of the UK. But suddenly there is a new item on everybody's to-do list, and it is not one anybody could have envisioned.

They all now feel invested in helping this poor woman find her missing child.

That's the simple explanation for the screaming. The woman who is so worked up is that way because she is a mother who cannot find her daughter and, under these circumstances, her reaction is entirely understandable. This is a busy public place, with lots of adults and children around, and as such, it is easy for somebody to get lost in the crowd. But the infant in question here has not simply got lost.

They have been taken.

As the desperate mother runs along the seafront, crying out for her baby while feeling like her world is imploding, the crowds part as she cuts through them, everybody trying to get out of her way because they don't want to be the one who delays this poor woman and prevents her from being reunited with her little girl as quickly as possible. But it doesn't matter that they allow her to pass, because the mother cannot find her child. The longer it goes on for, the less likely it seems that they will ever be back together again.

That realisation is enough to cause the frantic mother to drop down to her knees and weep. As she does, she thinks about how all the terrible things she has experienced in the past pale in comparison to this feeling right here.

The affair. The deaths. The police investigations. The revenge plots. As bad as all that had been, this is worse because she has been able to survive all of that and keep going.

But right here, it feels like it is all too much for her and that might mean only one thing.

Is it finally over?

BEFORE

ONE

FERN

The promenade is uncharacteristically quiet as I make my way along it, but that can be explained by two things. One, the weather is a little grey and blustery today, which is the reason the beach is devoid of any sunseekers at present. And two, it's a weekday morning, so all the locals are at work and all the tourists won't be arriving until Friday afternoon at the earliest. That's fine by me, because I'm not a fan of the crowds, for very obvious reasons.

A woman like myself, on the run from the law and living under a false identity, tries to avoid seeing too many people.

However, despite my unusual situation, I refuse to simply hide away forever, and that's not just for my own sake but the sake of my daughter too. She needs to interact with other human beings, which is why I have forced myself to leave my tiny flat and make my way to the rundown community centre at the other end of the seafront.

Looking down at the angelic face that peers up at me from the pram, I smile at my daughter, Cecilia, and feel the kind of feelings I never thought it was possible to have. My body is bursting with love for the little person I gave birth to only three months ago. I am overwhelmed by how much pressure and privilege I have to be the one tasked with keeping her safe. Being a mum was not always a dream of mine but, now that I am one, I couldn't be happier. Despite the rest of my life being in complete disarray, my child is providing me with that one beacon of hope that makes me think that perhaps, one day, everything just might turn out well in the end.

A large seagull suddenly squawks above my head, and I glance up to see the white bird circling below the ashen sky before it swoops down and lands a few feet ahead of me, instantly using its beak to peck at a discarded tray of chips dropped there on the ground by a tourist, presumably. The local residents know better than to litter, but those passing through on holiday don't tend to care quite as much, which is a shame, because this really is a beautiful coastal village and many people work hard to try and keep it as such – it's just the few that spoil it. As a resident of this village myself now, I am always careful to look after it, which is why I pause for a moment and, after shooing the seagull away, pick up the tray of leftover chips and toss them into a bin. Then I'm on my way again, pushing little Cecilia onwards to our destination, smiling at my gurgling girl while also feeling proud for doing my bit to keep this seafront looking so picturesque.

Having spent most of my life in Manchester – before a couple of short and best-forgotten stints in both Arberness in Northern England and London – I have landed here, in Bowey, a large village in Southern Cornwall and it is here where I intend to stay for the time being. I need stability, not just for Cecilia, but for my own good too, because there has been far too much upheaval in my world over the last year.

I arrived in Cornwall when I was halfway through my pregnancy with Cecilia, disembarking from the coach that had driven me from the city to the coast and making my way to my first night's accommodation with one hand resting on my growing bump and the other carrying the single suitcase that held everything I owned in the world. I was nervous, not to be in a new place but because I wasn't sure if the fake identification documents I had recently obtained were going to do the job of allowing me to begin a new life here. It was imperative they did because there was a lot I had to do. I needed to find a place to stay, I needed to seek child benefits so I could afford to feed and clothe the baby that was growing inside of me and, most importantly, I would have to attend numerous hospital appointments before my unborn baby was due. All those things had to happen, but they could only happen if I was able to start afresh under my assumed identity.

As I walk along this seafront, Fern Devlin feels very much a part of my past. I haven't operated under that name since I fled Carlisle just over a year ago after learning the police had evidence that would see me arrested for the murder of my ex-husband, Doctor Drew Devlin, not to mention be questioned over all the other crimes I had committed after that. I only have to look at my darling daughter to be reminded of one of those crimes. The truth is I murdered my baby's father, Greg, in cold blood, after discovering he had been lying to me. It turned out that, rather than being my boyfriend, he was actually just pretending to be in love with me and his real aim was to expose my crimes.

So far, Greg is the only person in the world who has drawn a confession from me about what I did to my late husband Drew, not that it did him any good in the end because he paid for that with his life. With my secret threatening to be exposed, I had to take drastic action and it was my life or his. I don't regret what I did because, without it, Cecilia might not be here now. The fact I must have conceived Cecilia just before killing

Greg means the little life we made together will only ever know one of her parents. Raising a child as a solo parent is something that's hard, but it was the only way I could save myself and my baby. I'd have preferred a different life for my child, one in which she had both her parents around to love her, but it was not meant to be. The main thing is that I'm in a position to care for her every day without interference from anybody else – most of all, the police.

I love Cecilia more than anything in the world and, as she grows, I know that she will love me.

At least she will as long as she never knows what I have done.

Like most things in my life, nothing has ever really gone to plan. From marrying a wealthy doctor who ended up cheating on me, to plotting Drew's demise with his mistress's husband, only to then have to finally kill my own husband. That was enough, but when I tried to start again, my new existence was ruined when I was exposed by Greg – the man I thought had fallen in love with me – so I had to kill him too. But I was too late and the police still discovered what I had done.

And it's only got crazier since.

Being guilty of so much and with the police closing in, I had no choice but to go on the run and that meant no longer using the name Fern, effectively killing off that part of myself in the process. I knew she could never be reborn because to do so would mean spending the rest of my life in prison. But now I have my fake ID documents, I have a second chance at life and it's one I intend to make the most of, for myself and my child.

The name now on my driving licence is Teresa Brown, though I've already been shortening it to Tess whenever I'm forced to introduce myself to anyone. That's the name everybody at the hospital knew me under when they were helping me deliver my baby, just like it's the name my landlord uses whenever he turns up demanding rent payments. It's also the name I will be giving today when I get to the community centre.

I'm on my way to a baby sensory class, an event where mums bring their babies for sixty minutes of playtime and inter-action. It'll be our first time attending such a class, which is why I'm a little nervous, but it should be fun. There'll be all sorts of songs sung, as well as various toys to pick up and play with and it'll be great for Cecilia's development. But I'm hoping it will also be great for my development too, in terms of me starting to build a network of people here who I might be able to call friends.

There's no doubt about it, being on the run is a lonely way of life, and I'm constantly in conflict with myself as to what I should be doing. But I know the safest course of action for me is to stay at home in my flat and avoid people all together, lest one of them figure out that I'm the infamous doctor's widow as reported on in the newspapers. Or – to use another name the journalists have given – *the Black Widow*.

I look a lot different to how I did when I first went on the run, having dyed and then cut my long hair, as well as taking to wearing much more dowdy clothing than I was previously accustomed to. That has all gone into helping me remain elusive. Barring going under the knife to have plastic surgery, there isn't much more I can do to alter my appearance, though I don't wish to be as drastic as that anyway. I don't desire to be operated on, not just because I can't afford it but because I'm keen to avoid any scary surgeries if I can help it. So far, no one has recognised me with the more superficial changes I have made and I am hoping I can keep it that way.

While I am pleased my new look and new way of living has kept me under the radar, I still long for my old way of life, the one where I could wear the clothes I wanted, style my hair the way I liked it and make myself look beautiful instead of just plain. I also long for the life where I had friends I could call and chat with, and had fun social events to attend at weekends. I miss all of that. Oh, what I would give to glam myself up and have a drink with a few mates and catch up on some gossip. More than that, I miss my parents, and it breaks my heart that I can't ever see them again, nor will they ever get to meet their gorgeous granddaughter. I'd love to see them with Cecilia, bouncing her on their knees and making silly faces at her. She has my father's smile and my mother's eyes, which is wonderful but also means I am constantly reminded of them whenever I look at her face. I can't decide whether it's better that Cecilia resembles my side more than Greg's, but it's probably preferable this way.

Better to look at my daughter and be reminded of my parents, rather than the man I murdered.

But it's tough to raise a child without the support of my parents, and even tougher to miss out on so much time with them myself. I'd love to have some precious adult time with them, be it as simple as a cup of coffee with Mum and a long walk with Dad, because we never know how long our parents will be around for, do we? But as time passes and my detachment to my old way of life only grows by the day, I know I can never go back and see any of them ever again.

It's simply too risky.

The bottom line is that I don't know anybody here, barring my doctor, my landlord and my next-door neighbour, and that's not much of a support network. Maybe today I'll meet another mum and we can become firm friends as we meet up regularly for playdates with our babies, setting the world to rights over cups of coffee or maybe even glasses of wine. My nervousness about possibly making a new friend is the reason I am lingering outside the community centre now. The old, confident me would have already walked through these doors by now with a big smile on her face, warmly greeting anybody she met before going on to have many interesting conversations with people who would be keen to see me again once they got to know me. The new me is very different, riddled with anxiety, self-doubt and almost preferring to be a wallflower than the centre of attention. There is no doubt it is going to be harder for me to make friends if I'm so self-conscious and afraid to open up to people, lest they figure out who I really am and what I'm hiding. I guess I'll have to try, or I'll be very lonely for a very long time.

However, I'm also aware that feeling lonely is a small price to pay for feeling free. As long as I'm not in handcuffs and able to raise my daughter myself then I can't complain too much.

But there is somebody out there who has every right to complain and that is Alice, my late husband's mistress and a woman who not so long ago was in handcuffs herself thanks to my plotting. I know the woman I framed for Drew's murder is out of prison now after her sentence was expunged, something that had to happen in the eyes of the justice system because she was innocent, but something that has caused me plenty of problems since. While Alice was behind bars, I was free to live as I pleased, residing in a spacious house in my home city of Manchester and feeling rather smug about having got away with murder and exacting the perfect revenge on both the husband who betrayed me and his attractive mistress. Now Alice is out and I'm the one who is living in purgatory, which is not how this was supposed to play out at all.

I still feel aggrieved by what Drew and Alice did behind my back; I'm still paying for it to this day. But what of Alice? Just because she is free, I don't assume she is happy. She did go through hell both in court and in prison before my lies were unravelled and, because of that, I have to assume she is intent on getting revenge. I'm sure she's out there now, dreaming of my downfall, plotting a way in which she can lead the police right to me and then get to witness my arrest and imprisonment. I know I would be doing exactly this if I were in her shoes.

Alice must be desperate to find me, but I'm just as desperate to stay hidden.

Only time will tell which one of us ultimately comes out on top.

The doctor's wife?

Or the doctor's mistress?

TWO

ALICE

I stare out of my window at Arberness and think about how this village in the north of England used to be different. It was once so quiet. Tranquil. Peaceful. It's no longer that way, or at least it isn't for me.

That's because these days all I can hear is crying.

Turning away from the window and the view of the outside world, which offers a freedom I can't quite relate to anymore, I see my angelic yet energy-absorbing child lying in her crib and let out a deep sigh when I do. My baby might look cute – currently still bald, though tufts of blonde hair are no doubt imminent because I'm blonde too – but she is hard work.

Evelyn is awake, again, and crying, again, and I feel utterly exhausted, *again*.

While I know I should approach the crib and attempt to sooth my distressed baby, I delay for a moment because it's only been ten minutes since I put her down to sleep. I haven't had anywhere near enough of a break from motherly duties in that time. I just want my child to sleep and, just as crucially, I want to sleep, but it seems neither are currently viable options. That's why, as I watch Evelyn, my eight-month-old, get to the point where she has tears in her eyes, I also feel like weeping too, simply out of fatigue and a desire to have a break from parenthood for just one day.

I never planned to have a baby and I certainly didn't plan to have Doctor Drew Devlin's baby. My affair with the doctor was a mistake from day one and led to all sorts of unexpected things happening, but Evelyn might just be the most unexpected one of them all. To say I was blindsided by my pregnancy would be an understatement. My ill-fated rendezvous with Drew in his doctor's office, after he had followed me to Arberness, had far-ranging repercussions that I never could have predicted at the time. Not only did that illicit meeting result in Drew's wife finding out that her husband was up to no good with me again, but it resulted in a little life starting to grow inside of me. The impact of that has almost been as life-changing as my false imprisonment.

Prison was tough but at least there I could get a few hours' consistent sleep. But now, living with a baby who refuses to rest, has me feeling like I am overwhelmed even more so than when I was facing years behind bars for a crime I didn't commit.

I know it's stupid to compare what I went through with Fern to being a new mum, but I'm so tired that I can't help it. My thoughts are as fuzzy as my eyes are bloodshot and, while I haven't actually admitted it to anybody yet, it's obvious what is going on here.

I'm seriously struggling.

As I continue to delay picking up Evelyn and soothing her, I think about how it's been difficult for me ever since she was born. I was told that babies sleep a lot in the first week or so after birth and then, in the following weeks, tend to get anywhere from twelve to sixteen hours rest in a twenty-four hour period. That has not been my experience; Evelyn hardly sleeps, never resting for more than half an hour at a time. This is just one of the many reasons why I feel both envious and angry when I read the articles online about new mothers who talk about sleep schedules and their babies who can go all night without being comforted. Social media has been another source of frustration for me because it just seems to be full of mums 'living their best baby life', sharing tips on how to have a child who sleeps through the night and who can be taken to restaurants or even on holiday without so much as making a fuss.

Really? Is it achievable? Could I get my baby to sleep more than thirty minutes at once or take her out in public without having her scream the place down? I don't know. Maybe. I'm simply too exhausted to even try.

I know I should feel lucky to have been blessed with a healthy child, but I also feel unlucky that it's been so tough, and that's even before my unusual life circumstances are taken into account. I am raising a fatherless child because Evelyn's dad died before we even found out we had conceived her, and that is a tragic circumstance that not many mums have to experience. I'm already dreading the day in the future when Evelyn starts asking me about her daddy, and I'm certainly dreading the day when she is old enough to read the news reports and learn exactly what happened to him and why. What kind of effect is it going to have on her in adulthood to go through life knowing that her father was murdered on a beach because her mother was having an affair with him behind his wife's back? I suppose my biggest fear is that by the time Evelyn is fully capable of looking after herself, she will tell me that she hates me and never wants to speak to me again. And that will make everything I am going through right here seem like a complete waste of time.

Of course, I want my child to love me, but with what I've done in my past, and the fact both her parents have been in the news so much, is that possible? Doesn't every child just want a stable home? Unfortunately, I can't give Evelyn that because there's nothing stable about me and the process I went through to end up having her. Nor do I expect there to be much stability on the horizon, certainly not with my fraught mental state.

The crying is only getting louder but I'm still doing nothing to rectify it, which is why the bedroom door opens and help arrives in the form of the third person I share this house with. It's my new boyfriend. He's a man who is already proving to be more adept at looking after a baby than I am, not that it takes much to beat me there. To fit in perfectly with my insane life situation, my new boyfriend is also the man who investigated Evelyn's father's death and foolishly helped put me behind bars for that crime, after he fell for Fern's lies. Eventually, he realised the error of his ways and helped secure my release. It's a man I learnt to forgive because we have something in common, and that thing is that Fern screwed over the both of us. It's also a man who has been a godsend since I found out I was going to become a mother, helping me both pre-baby and post.

It's Detective Tomlin.

'*Shh*, it's okay baby girl, come here,' he says as he reaches into the crib, his tie hanging down over my baby and her blanket, and his white shirt creasing as he picks her up. I remember this man looking rather shabby when I first encountered him not long after Drew's body had been found on the beach, but he has smartened up his appearance somewhat since. I guess he's done that for me, now he has somebody to impress, which I would appreciate more if I wasn't so goddamn tired all the time.

No sooner has he lifted Evelyn up than her crying stops. That's usually the way it goes – she just wants to be held – which would be cute if not for the fact that it is impossible to hold a baby for every hour of the day. But as my boyfriend cradles my baby and whispers sweet nothings to her, I wonder why he is able to make it look so easy, while I am finding it impossible.

As I watch Tomlin adequately perform duties that I seem incapable of performing myself, I feel all the usual amounts of shame, regret and sadness that I usually do when I realise I'm not turning out to be the perfect mother I thought I could be. But I also feel something else too. It's relief, because with him here it means I don't have to deal with the problem; that's why I leave the room, removing myself from the stressful situation.

'Are you okay?' Tomlin asks me when he sees me departing, before going back to shushing Evelyn, who is most likely going to require changing and feeding again now that she is up.

'Yeah, I'm just going to wash some bottles,' I say, and I head downstairs before there's any chance of Tomlin giving me the baby and offering to do the washing himself. The truth is I need a break and it's better to be in the kitchen doing boring chores than it is to be back in that bedroom where I have spent so many sleepless nights.

I should use this small window of time I have to be proactive and get to work on sterilising a couple of bottles in preparation for future feeds, like I just told Tomlin I would, but instead I simply slump down into a chair at the kitchen table and rest my head in my hands. It's Tomlin's day off today so I'm grateful for that, because it means I'm not having to do everything here by myself, but that still doesn't mean it's easy. What I'd give to be able to get out of here and go and do something that doesn't involve dirty nappies, burping or trying to calm a restless child. As it is, I'm essentially trapped, and that's why I sometimes think that I'm in a type of mental prison these days, as opposed to the physical prison I was in after Fern framed me.

Frustrated and teary, I bang my hands down on the kitchen table, but who am I kidding? I'm not just feeling this way because I'm struggling to adapt to my newfound responsibilities.

I'm feeling this way because the woman I hate is still out there now, free and living her life.

I still don't know where Fern is, nor do I understand how exactly she has been able to evade the police for as long as she has. What I do know is that every second she is free is another insult to what I have been through, and also to the memory of the men she has hurt along the way.

Fern is a serial killer, there is no other way to describe her.

She killed Drew because he was cheating on her, using my husband, Rory, as part of her plan.

She then killed Rory because she presumably thought he had become a liability to her.

Then, as if that wasn't enough, she killed Greg, an old friend of Drew's who was pretending to be her boyfriend while hoping to induce a confession out of her. He died, though not in vain, because the confession he secretly recorded and sent to Tomlin is the thing that allowed me to leave prison, so I'll be forever grateful for that. Although this is still far from resolved; Fern vanished after killing Greg and, so far, she is yet to resurface.

But she will. She can't stay hidden forever. She'll slip up. Make a mistake. Do something she shouldn't. Knowing Fern, she won't be able to help herself. She always had a taste for the good life and, while she might be struggling for a while, I doubt she'll stay that way for long. A woman like her is very persistent and very ambitious, and those two qualities might just end up being her downfall.

The problem for me is that it is already taking too long. The police don't seem to be getting anywhere with finding her, which is a big problem, because what if they give up looking? I'm telling myself that I'll feel better when she is found because then I can have closure, but will I get it?

It's scary to think that I might not.

In the meantime, I really need to sterilise these bottles while I have the chance.

That's because Evelyn is crying again upstairs.

I might just start doing the same thing in a minute.

THREE

FERN

As I'd hoped, Cecilia seems to love the sensory class. She smiles when I shake the brightly coloured maraca in front of her face, and she giggles when I hit the tambourine. Most of all, she's mesmerised when all the lights are turned out and a number of glowing stars are projected onto the ceiling, making it feel as though we're travelling through space rather than sitting in a darkened room in a worn-down community centre in Cornwall.

That's why, as the class ends and everybody gets ready to leave, I think this was definitely worth it for her, and I'd say it was definitely worth it for me too. I had to dip into my very limited funds to pay the admission fee for this class, but I can make small concessions like that for my daughter, sacrificing spending that money on myself, as any good parent would.

Just being around people was something I needed after spending so much time sitting with Cecilia in the flat we share, and while there wasn't much chance for conversation in amongst all the loud playing of various musical instruments, I did make some small talk with a few other mums. I'm confident they had no reason to doubt me when I gave them my fake name, nor when I told them my fake backstory. The story I'm telling is that I moved down here from up north after breaking up with Cecilia's father, and wanted to start a new life here because this was where I holidayed as a child and I'd always dreamt of living in the area one day.

While it has been so easy to toss and turn in bed at night and imagine a person seeing straight through my lies and then phoning the police to tell them that they have found the most wanted woman in the UK, the truth is that such a fear is not really realistic. I don't look like I used to, what with my new hair colour, distinct lack of makeup and penchant for wearing baggy, unstylish clothes as opposed to the trendier threads I used to be seen in. It also helps hugely that I have a baby with me because as far as the police know I'm just a single woman moving around alone. Nobody had any idea I was pregnant when I went on the run, so they aren't telling members of the public to be on the lookout for a single mum with a baby in tow. While I didn't keep Cecilia because I wanted that extra cloak of disguise, there is no denying her presence is helping me hide, because none of the newspaper reports mention me having a child. I hope it stays that way because maybe I'll never be found then.

However, what the newspaper reports have mentioned is that somebody connected to my case does have a baby, and to say it was a shock when I found out would be an understatement. While my baby might still be a secret, I know all about Alice's. According to the media reports, the father of her child is known to me too.

It's Drew.

It's just hearsay in the news because Alice hasn't spoken to any journalists herself and made it official, but they are all assuming the child she has been pictured pushing around Arberness was fathered by my late husband and the man she had an affair with before I nipped it in the bud so spectacularly. I suppose there is a chance Alice could have conceived with

Rory, her late husband, before his own demise, but that doesn't make for quite as good a story in the newspapers.

The Doctor's Baby

That headline gets more attention than any other could.

So what if it is true? Do I care that Drew has a daughter out there in the world and that Alice gets to be the mother to her? I tell myself no, but I'd be lying if I said I hadn't woken up in the middle of the night before and been troubled by it. But what can I do? I have my own baby to raise so I need to focus on her and, besides, Alice having a child might be a good thing. If she is busy being a mum, it might mean she is too busy to look for me.

As I make my way to the exit, Kirsty, a mum I briefly spoke to in the class, compliments me on my hair and asks me where I had it done. I freeze for a moment because the truth is this is a wig, though I obviously can't say that without it arousing suspicion.

'Oh, erm, a friend did it for me when she came to visit me,' I say. 'She's a hairdresser.'

'It's lovely,' the mum with the more expensive pram than me says and, for a second, I fear she is going to reach out and touch my hair, which really would threaten to ruin the illusion. She doesn't do that and my secret is safe as the conversation moves onto sleep schedules as we make our way outside. I'm wondering if I'm going to have Kirsty accompanying me all the way back to my flat. I hope not because I don't want her to see where I live; it's very undesirable. I'm spared any awkwardness though because she and her cute baby leave me halfway along the promenade, looking to turn down a street that I know is filled with very expansive and expensive homes. We say our goodbyes and that we're looking forward to seeing each other at next week's class. Then it's just me and Cecilia again. We arrive back at the flat I'm renting, which is certainly very different to where my new friend has just gone back to.

This is my home.

If I dare even call it that.

Just taking one look at the dreary place I now reside in is enough to fill my heart with sorrow, because if there is anything to show how much of a downfall I have suffered then it is this address right here. I'm currently raising Cecilia in a flat that is barely fit for having inhabitants, and as I take in the sight of the grotty environment around me, I let out a sad sigh.

The piles of bin bags outside some of the doors are as unsightly as the overturned shopping trolley lying on the ground. As I make my approach to my front door, the loud music I can hear emanating from one of the flats also does nothing to add to the ambience of this place. It's not unusual for that music to be blaring out long into the night, which is obviously just what the parent of a young child needs when it comes to bedtime.

As I push the pram deeper into this 'lovely' place, my eyes linger on an empty bottle of wine that rests against one of the dirty brick walls. I have to quickly avert my gaze when I accidentally make eye contact with a young man wearing a hood over his head. He looks like trouble but bizarrely I realise that, if we ever were to interact, I'd probably end up being the most dangerous one of the two of us.

Unlike most parts of this village, parts that are picture-perfect and adorn the front of postcards, this is one area that is very much unloved. It's a far cry from the decadent homes that sit atop the clifftops with sweeping views of the sea, and is a metaphorical million miles away from the grand properties with expensive cars sitting outside them on the driveway. It's certainly different to the types of places I have lived in the past, be it spacious houses in Manchester or a huge home in Arberness that offered fantastic views of the water literally just across the road from my front door. But times have changed, and this is all I can afford now, though hopefully not all I can afford forever.

As I reach the front door of my pokey flat, I take out my key and prepare to enter my very humble abode. But before I can, I hear the door next to mine unlocking before it opens and I see the smiling face of my neighbour, Victoria, emerge from within.

'Hi, Teresa! How's little Cecilia doing?' Victoria asks me. I smile too because it is nice to see a friendly face, especially one who adores my little girl.

'She's doing great, thank you,' I say as Victoria gets busy cooing over the top of Cecilia's pram, and I allow my neighbour the opportunity to have this fun interaction with my child.

Victoria is five years my junior, still some way off grappling with the concept of turning forty like I did not so long ago. She has a beauty about her that I felt I once possessed before I endured multiple sleepless nights as a new mum as well as all the stresses that come with being on the run. While I struggle daily with my current life situation, Victoria always seems positive and, with her bright eyes, dazzling red hair and wide smile, she is a real ray of light in this grim little section of the map. Of course, she knows absolutely nothing about the real me and, as far as she is concerned, I'm just a woman like her, slightly down on my luck and living here until I can get my finances, and indeed my life in general, in a healthier state.

'She's gorgeous,' Victoria says as she tickles Cecilia's cheek. My little girl likes it and I know this because she rewards our neighbour with a beautiful smile. That smile has only appeared over the last few weeks, but it melted my heart when I first saw it and it continues to do so to this day.

'We've just been to a sensory class, haven't we?' I say in that mumsy way in which I make conversation with an adult but talk as if I'm speaking to the baby.

Why do parents do that? I don't know but I'm no different.

'Wow, that sounds fun!' Victoria squeals, and it's always obvious that my neighbour loves our little chats. It takes a lot to brighten up a day in these flats, but a beautiful baby girl seems to do the trick. However, I could do with getting inside my own flat because I have some things to be getting on with, so I make that known to my neighbour in the politest way possible.

'I better get this one inside. I have a feeling there is a dirty nappy that needs changing,' I say and that always seems to do the trick in getting people to stop cooing over Cecilia and leave her to me again.

'Well, you two have a lovely day and I'll see you soon,' Victoria says, gushing over Cecilia one more time before finally stepping back from the pram and allowing us to enter our home.

Once I'm inside, the pleasant feelings from that friendly interaction on my doorstep quickly dissipate when I look around my dreary dwelling. This studio flat is as small as it is cheap and, as I lift Cecilia out of her pram, I then have to squeeze past said pram in the narrow hallway just to get into the main living quarters.

Far from being able to wander from room to room and take in all the different decorative themes and items of furniture like I had in my previous homes, almost everything here is contained to the same room. The living room, kitchen and bedroom are all essentially combined into one, meaning the only other room I have is the small bathroom through the door to my left. My bed is beside an armchair that sits opposite a kitchen countertop, and that's about it.

What little space there is has been filled with bags of fresh nappies and wet wipes. The one small area there used to be on the carpet by the armchair is now covered by Cecilia's changing mat. The impractically small fridge beneath the countertop compliments the crammed cupboards that are full of tins of soup and beans and any other cheap items I buy to sustain myself. While there used to be a little space at the foot of my bed when I first viewed this place, that is now taken up by Cecilia's crib. This place is so cramped that it makes me want to cry out or even scream sometimes, but that won't change my situation. All it would do is panic Cecilia or Victoria next door, if she heard me, and I don't want to do that. That's why, rather than have some sort of a nervous breakdown, I bite down on my lower lip before easing myself into the uncomfortable armchair and proceeding to breastfeed my baby.

As I look down at my beautiful daughter's face, I tell myself that she doesn't care where we live or how much money we have. All she wants is the love of her mother, and that I can give her, simply because it's free. That's lucky because it's about all I can give her at this time, although I'm hoping that can change soon. There is something I am working on, although I haven't made much progress yet. Speaking of a lack of progress, the *drip-drip-drip* sound coming from my kitchen tap is proof that my landlord has still not done what I have repeatedly asked of him and fixed the leaky appliance. That means I'll have to make another frustrating phone call to him to ask him again if he will kindly fulfil his duties and fix this issue for his down-on-her-luck tenant.

I hate speaking to Nigel, the creepy man in his sixties who owns this place, because when he's not making lewd remarks to me, he's telling me lies about how quickly he will get somebody to fix one of the many issues around this place. The only thing that could make living here a little more bearable would be if it was owned by a friendly person who treated me with respect. As it is, it's owned by a pervy, ageing man who is an incompetent landlord on a good day and a downright lecherous bore on a bad one. As a new mother, with dark circles under my eyes, leaking breasts and stretchmarks across my stomach, not to mention all the extra weight I put on in pregnancy and haven't lost yet, I'd assumed I wouldn't be getting much male attention for a while. But Nigel seems to have no qualms about me not looking at my finest. Whatever the case, he'd fall into bed with me if I gave him half the chance, not that I plan to. He might quite like it if I decide to pay one month's rent with my body instead of my money, but that will never happen. Unfortunately, paying with my money is only getting harder by the day; what funds I have left are rapidly running out and, soon, Nigel really will be making my life difficult.

It's that realisation that turns my thoughts away from the dripping tap and back onto my plan for the future. There might just be a way I can get my hands on some much-needed money, and it won't require me getting some minimum wage job while leaving Cecilia with Victoria, which I don't want to do even if she would make a good babysitter.

All it requires is me figuring out the password to the bank account.

It's the bank account in my late husband's name but, crucially, it is an account that the police don't know about, which is why they haven't frozen the funds inside it yet and, hopefully, they never will. It's an offshore account, set up by Drew because he once saw a way of reducing his ever-growing tax bill and, while I'm not sure exactly how much is in there, I know that if I can figure out the password to access it online, I can not only see the balance on screen but I will be able to figure out a way of withdrawing it.

It's going to be tough, but I have to tell myself that I can do it. Besides, I've already done some difficult things to get here. Obtaining my fake ID documents for example. That wasn't easy.

In fact, it was downright dangerous.

FOUR

FERN

Usually, when a woman finds out they are expecting a child, it leads to a period of self-reflection and an honest assessment of how prepared they are for the time when they have the added responsibility of a baby in their daily lives. I'm no different, and that is unfortunate, because it hasn't taken me long to realise that I am in no position to be a mother. If I'm caught by the police, it's likely that my child will be raised in protective services rather than by me. That's why I need to make some changes and fast.

The problem there is that my options are severely limited.

That's what being on the run tends to do for a person.

After being shocked by the positive pregnancy test that I took in the bathroom of this hostel just a few days ago, I have been reeling ever since. But I've not totally wasted that time because I have had the clarity required to try and be proactive and improve my situation. Having made my mind up to keep my baby, as I'm aware it might be my one and only chance to become a mother, I thought about what would usually happen to someone in my situation. The obvious answer is hospital appointments for scans, routine check-ups at the doctor's and numerous consultations with midwives as my due date drew nearer. However, all of this seems impossible considering the police would be contacted the second I gave my real name in any kind of medical institution. If I want to safely monitor the progress of my pregnancy – seeing my baby on screen during an ultrasound and having honest discussions with a midwife about how best to cope with my impending responsibility – then I need one thing.

A new identity.

I know such a thing won't come cheap, which is one problem, but the first problem is where I can go to obtain such documents. I need a false passport and driving licence as a minimum, but ideally I also need a National Insurance number and an NHS number if I am to take full advantage of the free medical care in this country that would be offered to an expectant mother like myself. Literally having no idea how to get such things, I turn to the place most people turn to when they want answers.

The internet.

Sitting one night at the shared computer in the communal lounge downstairs in the hostel, I simply type in the words 'how to get a fake passport' and the internet tells me quite simply that my best bet is the dark web. However, I have absolutely no idea how to access such a shady part of the internet where criminals seem to roam freely, so figure that I'm at a dead end.

Is there really nothing I can do about this?

I figure that might be the case until one of the male staff members at this hostel comes and speaks to me quietly a short time after I have finished using the computer.

'You know, you really should have deleted your search history,' the young man with the long hair and stubble says to me, and while he looks like your average backpacker who has ended up not just passing through here but staying a while to earn some extra money for his trip, that's not my concern. What is my concern is what he says next.

'I've been able to see exactly what you were looking at online,' he goes on, a slight smirk on his face as if he is some super computer hacker and not just a nosey guy who has taken advantage of the fact that I made a big oversight in not clearing my browser history on a shared device.

'I've just watched a film about a criminal being on the run and I was curious,' I say, poorly trying to make up an excuse, but rather than posing a threat to me, the bearded backpacker tells me he might be able to help.

'I've worked here for several months now and I've seen plenty of people like you come through here,' he says, smirking less and becoming more serious as he speaks. 'There are a few subtle differences, but you have much in common. You all keep to yourselves—you barely make eye contact with anyone. Oh, and you also leave hair dye stains in the sink.'

I feel a tightness gripping my chest as I realise that, despite thinking I've been clever, this man here has figured out I'm hiding from something and somebody. If he can figure it out, who else can?

'I don't know what you're talking about,' I try lamely but he quickly interjects.

'Drop the act because there's no need for me to hear it. I don't know who you are or what you've done, and frankly I don't care. All I do know is that you must have a good reason to be looking into getting fake documents and it just so happens that I can help you out with that.'

Part of me wants to continue denying that I am somebody in need of a fake ID but I can't ignore the potential lifeline he has just thrown out for me, so I say nothing and allow him to continue.

'I know a guy who can get you whatever you want to start

your new life,' he says, smiling now as if he's just offered me a way to buy some fresh fruit and not some illegal paperwork that could land us all in prison if the police ever found out about it.

Devoid of any other options, and figuring it was pointless to keep on lying, I said I would like that and that was how I came to meet Dmitri, or at least that was the name I was given for the man who could get what I wanted.

But if I could use a fake name, so could he.

When I go to meet Dmitri in his fifth-floor apartment in a modest tower block in North London, it's clear he really is a man who can get his hands on anything. I see plenty of piles of passports, dozens of decks of driving licences and numerous National Insurance cards lying around the place; Dmitri seems extremely proud of his fraudulent talents. He tells me he can get me whatever I need and after I have given him my list, he says it won't be a problem.

But something will be.

His price tag.

'Seven thousand pounds,' Dmitri says to me with a very straight face, his quoted price for all the things I need to be able to start afresh without fear of future reprisals.

'I don't have that,' I reply honestly. 'I would pay it if I could, but I can't.'

'Then you're free to leave. Good luck finding what you need elsewhere.' Dmitri is calling my bluff, believing that I need him more than he needs me, but I try to turn the tables on him and call his bluff too.

'What's stopping me from giving an anonymous tip off to the police about you and your little operation here?' I ask, my heart rate increasing as I make my thinly veiled threat to this master criminal. 'If I was to do that, you'd be arrested.'

I see just how bad of an idea this is when Dmitri's mood turns instantly dark.

'Do something like that and you'll end up worse off than

me, I assure you,' he growls and, aware that I'm alone with him in this flat and unlikely to be able to escape if he tries to hurt me, I drop the idea of threatening him quickly.

'Please. I don't have that much money,' I beg, returning to honesty.

Dmitri considers this for a moment while eyeing me up and down.

'You're a pretty woman, or at least I can tell that you used to be before you did whatever you did and had to hide,' he says. 'That's why I'm willing to make a concession. Five thousand pounds. That's the absolute lowest I can go to. Take it or leave it. But remember, if you give me that money, you can get on with the rest of your life in peace.'

Grateful for the discount and aware that it's the best I am going to get, I am left with little choice.

'I'll get you the money,' I say defiantly while not quite knowing exactly how I am supposed to do that. 'Just make me the documents and I'll be back with it. I swear.'

That was yesterday and, since then, I've spent every hour racking my brains as to how I can come up with the requisite funds so I can get what I need and get my life in some semblance of order before my baby is born. Unfortunately, as of yet, I have no credible ideas.

I'm currently lying on my bed in the crowded hostel room in London, where I'm living as I continue to try and evade the police, the media and any members of the public who might recognise my photo from the front covers of all the newspapers in the supermarkets at the moment. I'm facing the wall with my back to everyone else in the room and pretending to be asleep but I'm wide awake, my mind tormented with fear and angst about the future, and that is why I can hear the conversation going on in the room around me.

With this being an eight-bed dorm room designed with budget-conscious international travellers in mind, privacy is not an option. Despite being desperate for some peace and quiet, I'm currently listening to three American backpackers in their twenties talking about all the fun they are anticipating as they begin their travels around Europe. By the sounds of it, it promises to be a fun trip because, from what I can gather, after London, they are planning on visiting such fantastic cities as Paris, Rome and Athens, amongst many others. That tells me it also promises to be an expensive trip, and it doesn't take much for me to wonder how these three Americans who seem so young in comparison to me are able to fund such an adventure. But I get my answer as I continue to listen to the trio of excited travellers talking. There's only the four of us currently in the room and, as I'm guessing they assume I am asleep, they are talking freely.

That's how I learn something that might be of use to me.

One of the women is talking openly about how her parents have paid for her to go on this trip and how much spending money they have given her while she is undertaking it. Her friends' jealousy is piqued when she tells them that her father has given her thousands of pounds and she currently has much of that money on her now because she thought it would be cool to see how much of it she could hide on her person through the airport. But that's not all that is piqued because, as she keeps bragging, my attention is very much on her tale of privilege; she might just be providing me with the answer to all my problems.

The boastful woman's friends are clearly envious, although they hardly seem like they are from disadvantaged backgrounds themselves, and one of them suggests they go out to a casino and spend some of their money having a night of fun. They even explore the idea of meeting a rich English gentleman like the ones they have seen in the movies, a Hugh Grant or Jude Law type, who charms with his eloquent accent and his cheeky smile. But the wealthy woman reminds them they have an early start in the morning, so they better get some sleep, though she does promise them a very wild evening in the nightclubs of Paris when they get there soon, all on her father's dime, of course.

With all their money, I do wonder why these three chose to stay here and not in some fancy hotel, but I'm guessing it's so that when they go home and see their friends, they can claim to have had the 'true backpacker experience' and it's one that isn't quite possible if you're sleeping in five-star resorts throughout it. That's fine by me and, as I continue to lie with my back to the women, I hear them getting ready for bed before the light goes off in the room.

After half an hour, I'm pretty sure all of them are asleep.

Slowly rolling over to look at them, I see their silhouettes in the darkness, three bodies resting peacefully beneath the thin sheets that came with the thin mattresses that adorn the bunkbeds in this cheap place. It takes me several more minutes before I have plucked up the courage to get out of my bed. After quietly getting dressed and gathering up my belongings, I feel like I am ready.

All I need to do now is see if I can find any of that money that bragging tourist allegedly has in her possession.

Creeping towards the backpack that lies on the floor beside the bed of the woman who I think is the one with the wealthy father, I am well aware that my plan will be ruined should any of these women wake up and catch me snooping around their belongings. Not only would my chance at taking their money be gone but they'd probably call the police and, while I'd run, could I get away again? But I'm desperate so I'll take that risk. Slowly unzipping the backpack, I cautiously reach inside and feel around for anything that feels like a wedge of cash. There are plenty of clothes in here, but it's when I lay my hands on the bulky envelope that I think I might have just found what I'm looking for.

Cautiously removing the envelope, I take a quick peek

inside and see £20 notes, which is all I need to send me tiptoeing away from the sleeping backpackers and towards the door. Only once I am out of the room do I really look inside the envelope and see how much I have just got.

It's a lot.

But it's still not quite enough.

With the £3,000 in this envelope, combined with what I have left, I'll still be some £700 short of the figure Dmitri quoted me, but there's not much else I can do to get any closer to it, so I'm hoping this will be enough. Surely he won't turn down all this cash if it arrives on his doorstep, so I intend to go to his apartment now and put that theory to the test.

Leaving the hostel and knowing I can never go back there, there is a part of me that feels guilty for stealing that woman's money. But then, after hearing how spoilt she was, my sympathy wanes, and while it's a sizeable sum that I have taken from her, I have a feeling it will only take one phone call to her father and the missing funds will be replaced quickly. Besides, I have taught her a valuable lesson and it's one she will do well to remember as she continues on her travels throughout Europe.

Be very, very protective of your belongings while living in shared accommodation with a bunch of strangers.

After taking the tube to the north of London, I make the rest of my journey to Dmitri's apartment on foot and by the time I arrive there, it's past midnight and I'm wondering if he will answer the door when I press the button that will sound the buzzer in his apartment. He does and, when I tell him that I have his money via the intercom, he lets me inside and suddenly, I feel like my dream of being able to start afresh under a new alias and raise my unborn child in peace is not such an impossible one anymore. That dream quickly fades when Dmitri tells me I am still short of his fee, and he isn't willing to reduce it.

Unless...

'No, absolutely not,' I say after he has just made his suggestion that the pair of us go into his bedroom to 'make up the
difference', but Dmitri doesn't like that answer and steps
towards me, looking menacing and reminding me that it will be
very dangerous to mess with a man like him. I think about just
grabbing the documents he has already made for me and
running for the door, but this won't be as easy as stealing from
that American backpacker just was. I realise I'm going to have
to be smart about this.

If not, I might never leave this apartment alive.

'Okay, I'll do it. Let's go to the bedroom,' I say, swallowing
my pride and giving the man standing in front of me the answer
he wants.

'I knew you'd say yes when you'd had a moment to think
about it,' he says with a satisfied smile while wagging his finger
at me. 'You're too desperate to give up your chance at freedom.'

With that, Dmitri turns and heads for the bedroom and I
reluctantly follow him. But as the bed comes into view, I feel
disgusted at this man and his means of conducting business. I'm
almost as disgusted when, having spotted a baseball bat leaning
against the door to his bedroom, I pick it up and seizing the only
opportunity I might have to alter my fate, I swing it at Dmitri's
head and hear him cry out as he falls to the floor.

The sound of the bat cracking against his skull was sicken-
ing, but I feel just as sick when I think about what will happen
to me if I don't get out of here before the stricken man is back on
his feet. I can scarcely believe what I've just done, though I had
clearly reached a tipping point. Sick of being pushed around by
men, from my cheating husband to my lying former boyfriend, I
reacted instinctively, seizing back control.

But it's not over yet.

Running back to where my falsified documents lie on his
living room table, my heart is thumping as I grab them as well as
the money I just paid him. Then, not slowing down for a

second, I rush for the door, determined to get out of here before Dmitri gets back to his feet, and while he calls me all sorts of horrible names, I make it out of his apartment while he is still recovering from the blow I dealt him.

There's a very nervous moment as I fail to find the door that will lead me to the staircase and, for lack of a better option, I'm forced into pushing the button for the elevator. It's a very tense wait for it to arrive to take me back down to the ground floor and, by the time it has got to me, I see Dmitri burst out of his apartment with blood pouring from his head. But the doors to the elevator slide shut just before he can reach me and, despite him most likely taking the staircase down to try and catch me up, I make it to ground level before he does. Once I'm out on the street, I am able to lose him easily in the city, aided by the darkness that accompanies this late hour.

I've done it. I've got what I need. I can start a new life under a new identity.

That means I've done what I had to do to be the best mother I can be to the child I'm carrying.

Isn't that all a mother can do?

Then again, most mothers don't leave a trail of death and destruction wherever they go, do they?

FIVE

ALICE

Overwhelmed at the pressure that comes with trying to be the perfect mother, I've left my house and left my baby at home with my boyfriend. Tomlin is with Evelyn and, while he wasn't happy about me going out, I told him I had to do it because I need a break. I wasn't lying, but he would have preferred it if I'd stayed, and we could have talked about things. He can clearly see that I'm struggling with the baby and, if he could have his way, he would have me discussing the possibility that I might be suffering with postnatal depression. For now, I am intent on avoiding any difficult conversations like that, which is why I've left home and am making my way into the centre of Arberness.

The village is quiet, as it always has been, barring that dark period of time when Drew's body was found on the beach here and this place was overrun with police officers and journalists. Sometimes, those days feel a long time ago, but at other times it feels like it was only yesterday when Arberness became the most talked about place in the UK. I sure am glad to see these streets back to being as sparsely populated as they should be and, without the sight of police cars or media vans parked at the kerb, there is a much more peaceful ambience about the place.

However, while things are quiet as I make my way into the centre of the village, I still feel like I can hear Evelyn's cries coming from her crib. I know that's not possible because there's enough distance between me and my house now to be out of earshot, but it's almost like I am hearing phantom cries. It's probably because, having heard little else but my baby screaming at the top of her lungs over the last few weeks, my brain is playing tricks on me and making me hear that same thing even when it's not really there. That tells me I definitely needed a break, and the coffee morning I am on my way to is providing me with the ideal opportunity to get that little escape I so desire.

I'm on my way to the church hall, which is the venue for the weekly village coffee morning, and it will be good to do something that used to make up part of my normal weekly routine. While I no longer am the one responsible for setting up for the meeting and making sure the attendees are well catered for like I used to be, it will be nice to walk in there and see some familiar faces belonging to the women in this village. I used to love running this event every week, but that had to stop when I was sent to prison, and it took me a while after my release before I felt comfortable going back. I thought people might gossip about me but, thankfully, when I did show my face again, everybody was extremely kind. That's why I'm feeling optimistic as I reach the church hall and walk inside to see some friends.

I spot some of the locals I recognise as soon as I enter, and I wave at Dorothy and Ethel, two kindly women who offer me warm smiles before coming over to check on my wellbeing. They ask me all about Evelyn and tell me that I must be having the most wonderful time as a new mum, so I just fake it and say that yes, it's a dream come true and I'm loving every minute of

it. Then they ask me how I am doing, and I know they are referring to my current state of mind after all the drama I went
through in the past year with Fern.

'I'm okay,' I lie. 'It's been hard, but things are getting a little
easier now.'

'I can't imagine how difficult it has been for you, and with a
new baby as well,' Dorothy says.

'You must be Superwoman,' Ethel adds, which is a statement that should make me feel better about myself but actually
only makes me feel worse, because I know how far from the
truth it really is.

'I don't know about that but I'm getting there,' I say with a
fake smile.

If only I believed that though, and, as I look around the
room, I'm struck by the memory of the time when Fern came
here posing as a new resident in the village who was looking to
make friends. Having to make small talk with the woman whose
husband I was having an affair with was painful and I hated
every second of it, but I hate the memory of that day even more
now because, in hindsight, I know that Fern was simply playing
games with me. Unbeknownst to me at the time, she knew
exactly who I was and what I had been up to with her husband;
her being here and befriending me was all part of her plan.
That plan went on to involve her inviting me and my husband
to her house for dinner, and that excruciating meal I had to sit
through will live long in the memory too. Fern was clever and
she deceived me, just like she deceived plenty of other people
for a long time, most notably the police, and being here is only
serving to remind me of that woman and the games she played
in this village.

I've often wondered if it has been a bad idea for me to stay
here, in this place that is full of reminders of my grim history.
But I've been far too overwhelmed to add a house move to my
to-do list, and that extra stress in my life would probably be the

straw that broke the camel's back, so I've remained here, for now, anyway. But one thing is for sure; while I am in Arberness, the ghosts of the past will continue to haunt me.

As I pour myself a cup of coffee and take my seat on one of the plastic chairs that has been arranged into a circle, I am regretting coming here; maybe I wasn't ready for this. I'm regretting it even more when I see who I have ended up sitting next to. Because on my left is Agatha, a woman who's never been a cheerful soul. I remember she sat next to Fern on the first day the doctor's wife came to this gathering but, if memory serves me right, Fern did spend a lot of that meeting looking in my direction. Back then, I just thought it was because I was the only woman in the room who was of a similar age to her, so she was thinking I was more 'new friend material' than some of the other attendees at the coffee morning who were in the older age range. Now I know that she was simply watching me because she saw me as the enemy and, like the old saying goes, 'keep your friends close but your enemies closer'. Just as I'm steeling myself for what will most likely be a dreary conversation with Agatha, I see who it is taking a seat in the empty chair on my right. It's Audrey, another familiar face, but also somebody who was close to Fern back when she lived here.

How close was she exactly?

They were next-door neighbours.

Managing to politely extricate myself from the conversation with Agatha, I turn to Audrey. When she realises that I am here, I see a sadness come over her. But I don't want pity and sympathy, because I already feel damaged enough without being made to feel like even more of a victim. So, before she can ask me how I am, I ask her that question instead. I had heard she'd been struggling coming to terms with the fact that she had lived in such close proximity to a woman who turned out to be a serial killer. Audrey had been inside Fern's house too and fallen for her charade, and such a close brush with a monster can end up having a profound impact on a person's mental health. I should know.

'I'm okay, dear. I've put all that terrible business behind me and am refusing to let what that woman did spoil my enjoyment of this village and all the wonderful memories I made here before *she* arrived.'

I don't fail to detect the extra emphasis she put on the word 'she' and I have no problems with it, because the disdain Audrey clearly has for Fern is music to my ears.

'How are you doing?' Audrey enquires then and I end up being more honest with her than I was with the others.

'It's tough. I feel like I can't relax until they've caught her,' I admit.

'Have the police given you any kind of an update recently?'

'No. There's been a few false leads, but nothing else.'

'It's disgraceful. What are they doing?'

'I don't know.'

Audrey is just as angry as I am that Fern is still at large, I can see that by the way her blue eyes narrow as she speaks with the wrinkles on her face becoming even more pronounced.

'That woman is a danger to the general public and the sooner she is locked away, the better,' Audrey goes on. 'To think that she could have infiltrated some other poor community by now and be hurting others. It makes me sick.'

'You and me both,' I say before I take a sip of my coffee. The caffeine does go a little way to improving my mood, though I know there's no amount of it in the world that can get me through another sleepless night with Evelyn. I came here to forget about my hard work at home, so I focus on enjoying the coffee morning, which I feel like I am doing a pretty good job of right up until my phone rings. I check the caller ID. When I see who it is, I leap out of my seat and, after quickly excusing myself, I rush to the edge of the room, answering the call where I can speak out of earshot of the other women.

'What is it? Have you found something? Is she in Southampton?' I ask in hushed tones of the man at the other end of the line.

'Not quite. I'm just calling you with an update. Unfortunately, the woman I suspected of being Fern is not her.'

'Damn it!' I cry and, despite planning on keeping my voice down, I end up erupting and all the women sitting in the circle on the other side of the room hear me.

I put up a hand in apology as they all look at me with concerned expressions on their faces before I go back to the caller.

'This has been a waste of time. You're not getting results, so I won't be sending any more money. Just forget it!'

I hang up then before the man has any chance at a comeback and, for a second, I feel like throwing my phone to the floor. But that would only draw even more attention to myself, and considering everyone is still looking at me, I should probably try and calm down.

'Sorry about that,' I say as I go to retake my seat. Perhaps because they all know of my troubled past, nobody dares press me for details as to what the call might have been about. That's good because I'd rather not say.

I'd rather not tell them I hired a private investigator to try and track down Fern, only to have to fire him after he failed to produce the goods.

As multiple conversations resume around me, I think about how I've spent over £2,000 on investigators since I gave up waiting for the police to find Fern and took matters into my own hands. That was money I could have spent on myself, my baby, my home or even just paid for a holiday so I could have got out of Arberness for a while. Instead, I've transferred it to a person who promised me they would find Fern and help bring her to justice sooner, yet despite their best efforts she remains hidden. The last time I spoke to the investigator who I just dismissed so brutally, he told me he was heading to Southampton to chase a lead but, once again, it's come to nothing. I'm not sure how much more money I want to invest in this frivolous and, so far, fruitless pursuit of the woman who wronged me. If only the police would do their damn jobs then I wouldn't have to hire freelancers, but here I am, desperate and trying anything I can to stop Fern in her tracks. But I'm discovering why the police haven't made any inroads in finding Fern. She's very elusive, and as I've seen with Tomlin, sometimes, simply trying your best to achieve a desired outcome doesn't mean you can actually get it.

I'm so lost in my thoughts that I don't notice the coffee morning meeting has come to an end until Audrey taps me lightly on the shoulder and asks me if I'm okay. I tell her I am before making an excuse and leaving. As I go, she tells me to give Evelyn a hug from her.

I say I will but I won't be doing that.

I don't want to think about home until I get there.

I'm dreading being back in that house listening to Evelyn's cries.

I need a break from all of this. I feel trapped.

I wonder if Fern feels the same way.

Living life on the run, surely she has to.

SIX

FERN

After another futile evening spent trying to correctly guess the password to Drew's offshore bank account, and yet another night of broken sleep thanks to Cecilia waking me up by making all sorts of strange noises in her crib, I was hoping that I could have a relaxing day today. My plan was to stay in all day, nap when I can and generally maintain a low profile. As is usually the case with a baby, plans regularly change, and that is why instead of staying in my flat, I am getting ready to go out again.

But this won't be a fun trip.

Having noticed Cecilia felt warm this morning, I've been monitoring her temperature for the last few hours and, worryingly, it seems to be on the rise. A quick phone call to the local doctor's surgery has resulted in them telling me that it's probably nothing but, if I'm anxious, I can bring my baby in for a quick check-up. I doubt I'm the first mother to opt for the safe option rather than leave it and risk it, so I said I would bring Cecilia in so she could be quickly looked at. Despite not wanting to go, I know I need to be on the safe side and get my daughter checked, just in case she is ill and requires medication.

Unfortunately, a trip to the doctor's means another opportunity for my lies to be unravelled and my true identity to be exposed. I tell myself that nobody here has doubted me so far, so everything will be okay today. Hopefully, the doctor won't ask me too many questions and will just be focused on giving the best care he can to Cecilia and, fingers crossed, this should just be a five minute appointment and I'll be back home again before I know it.

Leaving my flat, I'm praying that Victoria doesn't come out to say hello because I'm already running late and am due at the doctor's in ten minutes despite it being more like a twenty-minute walk from here. Thankfully, there's no sign of her. What there is, however, are numerous empty beer cans and cigarette butts littering the floor outside my door, and it looks like some of the local youths had a fun night out here last night, sitting around drinking and smoking and generally making this untidy area even untidier. I heard a few of them playing music just after midnight last night, but I knew better than to go out and ask them to keep the noise down. I know one of my neighbours tried that once because I heard her shouting at them to be more respectful, but their only retort to that was to throw a load of eggs at her front door, which told me I'm better off just leaving them to it.

I push the pram to the unassuming doctor's surgery, chatting to Cecilia as I go because I read online that it helps the baby's development if you converse with them, even though there's obviously not much coming back at me at this stage. Cecilia isn't her usual self and doesn't show me any smiles or make any giggling noises along the way, which only makes me feel more justified in my concern as I arrive at the doctor's and let the receptionist know we are here.

After taking a seat in the quiet waiting room, I try to keep Cecilia occupied as best I can but I'm also trying to keep myself occupied too because, in a setting like this, it's impossible to not be reminded of Drew. As an esteemed doctor, this was his natural habitat, a place where ordinary members of the public bring their health worries and pray that the person with all the medical knowledge and experience can tell them that everything is going to be okay. People put their lives in the hands of doctors every day all over the world, their fates decided by a multitude of options, be it the issuing of a prescription, a friendly diagnosis that the new symptom is nothing to worry about or, most worryingly, an urgent referral for further investigation. Like most people, I've never enjoyed a trip to the doctor's, my mind often irrationally filling with all sorts of scary visions of me being diagnosed with some deadly disease and being told I won't make it to my next birthday, even if the symptoms I'm presenting with seem to already be responding to mild antibiotics. I try to be practical, but it's impossible to not let paranoia take over, and now I have someone other than myself to worry about. I'm imagining Cecilia has some tropical fever that only one in a million babies ever contract and, any moment now, the doctor here is going to call for an ambulance. Realistically, that's not going to happen, and I know most patients who visit their local doctor's surgery turn out to be absolutely fine. I know that because Drew told me that was the case. He must have seen thousands of people during his long and mostly distinguished career in medicine, and he sometimes made a comment to me about how the majority of those people had basically been wasting his time when they came to see him.

'Another fun-filled day with a bunch of hypochondriacs,' was a comment Drew made from time to time when he got home from work, dropping his briefcase down, wearily unfastening his tie and opening the fridge in search of a cold beer. Even though he sometimes made out like he wasn't enjoying his job, I know he loved it really. It's because he had that one thing that none of his patients had when they came to see him.

He had power.

He could set their mind at ease with a warm smile and a

polite explanation of a common medical ailment, and I know he enjoyed wielding that power. He certainly enjoyed it when it came to dinner parties, where he got to appear all big and clever when people found out what he did for a living. The power in his job extended beyond his office and out into society, putting him at the top of the hierarchy in many a social situation. He wasn't the only one who enjoyed that power, because I liked it too.

Revelling in the respect such a noble profession garnered for both me and my partner was a thing I liked doing, be it at a glitzy event or simply when I was answering questions about my marriage while doing something as simple as taking out an insurance policy. Drew's lofty title elevated me too, allowing me to ascend to a higher rung of society's ladder, and while I also made sure to never become a snob or look down on others, I enjoyed the rarefied air that came with having a man on my arm as successful as Drew was.

Being a doctor's wife when things were going well.

Those were the days.

Alas, those days are long gone, and as Cecilia's name is called out by the male doctor we are seeing today, I get up from my seat and carry my baby in for one of the first but definitely not one of the last check-ups in her life.

This doctor is not as handsome as Drew was, not quite as dashing with a stethoscope around his neck, nor quite as commanding a presence as my late husband as he stands in front of me and smiles. He looks pleasant enough and really all I care about is if he can tell me whether the temperature my daughter is running is anything to worry about or not.

'Let's have a little check, shall we?' Doctor Morgan says after he has got me to place Cecilia on the bed in the corner of his room. As he checks her temperature, I step back, giving him the space he needs to work. But as I stand there, I can't help but have an awful flashback to another doctor's office like this one, and another bed in the corner of the room. That's because it was in Drew's office in Arberness where I overheard him making love to Alice. That was the moment I found out his affair was back on, ultimately causing me to put my extreme revenge plot into motion.

Who knows what would have happened if I hadn't gone to my husband's workplace that night to check up on him? Maybe things could have been different. Drew might still be alive now. I probably wouldn't be living here in Cornwall under a fake name and hoping this doctor doesn't pry too much into my medical background after he has finished treating my child. Life could have turned out very differently. But what's done is done and considering I have come out of it all with a beautiful daughter, I wouldn't want to change anything that might have affected that.

'Teresa?'

I'm snapped out of my daydream by the doctor trying to get my attention.

'I'm sorry. What?'

'I was just saying I don't think it's anything to worry about. Keep an eye on her, make sure she's well hydrated. But I think she'll be just fine.'

'Oh, okay. Great!'

That sounds good and, as Doctor Morgan steps back from the bed, I rush in and pick Cecilia up before she can get too fussy about being put down in the first place. Instead of this appointment being over, the doctor turns his attentions to me.

'So baby is fine. How is Mum doing?' he asks me and while it's a kind, genuine question I immediately feel nervous because I didn't come here to talk about myself.

'Me? Oh, I'm fine, thanks,' I reply before turning for the door.

'Is there anything you'd like to talk about?'

'Excuse me?'

I freeze before I've made it to the door. What does he mean by that?

'Being a new mother is tough. I was just wondering how you were getting on and if you needed to talk. Contrary to popular opinion, us doctors do actually care about people.'

Doctor Morgan chuckles at his own joke then. I force a smile onto my face but I'm still extremely uncomfortable. This is why I wanted to stay in my flat all day. Nobody can try and get me to open up if I'm on my own.

'I'm fine, thank you,' I say. 'I mean, I'm tired and a little stressed but it's nothing I can't handle. I hardly thought having a baby would be a walk in the park.'

'Well, if you're sure. My door is always open if you want a chat. I know that all your attention is on Cecilia here, which is only natural, but don't forget to take care of yourself too. The most important thing your daughter can have as she grows is a happy mother.'

I thank the doctor again for his kind words and relax a little; I can see he is just being nice and not digging for information into my background because he suspects me of being a fugitive. Then I leave and it's only once I am outside on the street again with Cecilia back in her pram that I can relax a little more, my heart rate slowing and that now-familiar tightness in my chest reducing once again. It's hard but I don't think there will ever be a time when I'm not stressed about someone exposing me. I know that's going to make it impossible for me to ever have an honest, heartfelt conversation with another person ever again, but that's simply the only way it can be.

I am aware things might be easier for me outside of England, where fewer people are likely to know me and my story and be on the lookout for *the dreaded doctor's wife*. Although it's one thing to think about going abroad and it's another to actually get there. As of yet, I haven't seriously considered taking my chances at border control and trying to flee overseas. But it is an option for me, albeit a risky one, and it is something I might do when Cecilia is a little older and I feel like I might not need the free healthcare services in this country quite as much. But of course, anything can happen, and my hand might be forced at any time, so never say never.

As I make my way home, I remember I could do with picking up a couple more packs of nappies because the supply at home is starting to dwindle so I call in at the supermarket. I also figure the extra ten minutes we are out of the flat won't do any harm for Cecilia who is starting to fall asleep in her pram as I push her around.

I find the nappies I need on aisle four and drop them into my basket hanging over one of my arms. I'm just about to walk on when I notice a man watching me at the other end of the aisle. He quickly averts his gaze when he sees that I have caught him peeping at me and that only makes me feel more suspicious of him. Deciding to just get on the move as quickly as I can, I walk in the opposite direction to him and make it onto a different aisle as I head for the checkouts at the front of the store. But as I get there, I notice the man again at the end of another aisle and he is still looking at me, which is now starting to send my paranoia into overdrive.

Does he know who I am? Has he been following me? Is he an undercover police officer? Are the rest of his colleagues waiting for me outside? Am I going to be arrested as soon as I set foot outside this supermarket and have to watch Cecilia be whisked away from me as I'm bundled into the back of a van and driven straight to prison?

My sweaty palms are causing me to lose my grip on the basket I'm carrying, but dropping my groceries is the least of my worries as I contemplate how this might be the end for me.

'Hi, can I help you?'

The query from the smiling employee manning the checkout forces me to do something other than daydream about scary scenarios; I place the nappies on the conveyor belt, allowing her to scan them for me. While she does that, I glance back in the mysterious man's direction, but I can't see him now.

Where has he gone?

Looking all around me, I fail to find him, and I have to stop looking and get my purse out when the member of staff tells me how much I owe her.

Dipping into my dwindling funds, I pay for the nappies before chucking them into a shopping bag and then putting them in the basket at the bottom of the pram. Then, after one more look around to make sure that man is no longer watching, I head for the exit as quickly as I can.

Maybe it was nothing. Maybe he was a nobody. Hopefully, I'll be alright.

Then I step outside the supermarket and see the man is waiting for me.

'Hi,' he says and every muscle in my body is tense as I wait for him to call me by my real name and tell me the game is up.

After I've failed to respond to him, the man glances at Cecilia before he speaks again.

'Sorry, I don't usually make a habit of this, and I can see you're busy. I was just wondering, would you like to go for a drink sometime?'

Wait, what? That's it? He's asking me out on a date? All that staring was just him trying to pluck up the courage to come and talk to me?

'I'm sorry?'

'A drink? Or a coffee, if you can't get a babysitter. Whatever's easiest. I just thought, maybe, if you would like, we could meet up sometime.'

Wow, it really is just a guy asking me out on a date. Sleep-deprived, rushed-off-my-feet me. It's laughable that he would find me attractive in my current state but it's certainly preferable to him being a police officer knowing who I really am.

'I'm sorry. I've not really got the time for anything like that at the moment,' I say before I smile politely and then push the pram onwards, leaving the unlucky-in-love man standing alone at the supermarket door.

It's only when I get back to the flat that I can laugh about the fact that somebody tried to pick me up while I was out buying nappies with a baby in tow. However, the laughter soon fades when I remember that, for me, dating, relationships and even just fun in general are probably off the cards for a long time, if not forever. That's enough to stop the laughing and, while Cecilia hasn't cried for a few hours now, I feel like I might just be about to shed enough tears for the both of us.

That brief interaction with the plucky man who simply wanted to take me on a date is proof that I'm not like everybody else. I can't do the things they do. I'm not normal and I never will be.

The life I had is over.

The life I'm left with can never be considered to be full.

SEVEN

ALICE

As the sun goes down and another potentially restless night draws nearer, I am glad Tomlin is here to help with Evelyn. I've been in a terrible mood ever since firing my private investigator for lack of progress in finding Fern, and that is why I can't face being left alone to look after a baby. My boyfriend has no idea about me hiring a PI though, which means he just assumes my dark mood is down to me being overtired, which is also true. I might have done well to keep a secret from a deducing detective, especially one living in the same house as me, but then again, maybe not. Tomlin is almost as sleep deprived as I am and, considering he has a busy job to go to on top of dealing with mine and Evelyn's problems, it's probably safe to say he doesn't have much bandwidth left for discovering that I've been doing something sneaky behind his back.

But it's not just him who doesn't know about my penchant for PIs lately. I haven't told anybody that I've been paying good money for supposed experts to track down the woman who framed me for murder because I have a feeling that, at best, they would try and talk me out of it and, at worst, they would think I have a dangerous obsession with getting revenge and am not acting in a healthy way. I've tried several PIs recently and none of them have helped, unless by helped I mean they only added to my general state of distress and frustration. But as I replay that phone conversation again in my head, the one in which my useless PI told me that Southampton had turned out to be a dead end, I am not concentrating on what I am doing, which is why I almost end up lowering Evelyn into a bath full of boiling water.

'What are you doing? It's too hot!' Tomlin cries, shooting out an arm and preventing Evelyn's feet from coming into contact with the water I just poured. Suddenly, I'm snapped out of my daydream and realise that he is right. We have a yellow rubber duck that we put in the bath and, while it looks like a cute toy, it also doubles as a thermometer, displaying the water temperature and helping us get it to thirty-seven degrees, the temperature advised for babies. Any hotter than that and it could burn Evelyn; because I wasn't paying full attention to what I was doing, I hadn't seen that the rubber duck was flashing red and that the water temperature is well over forty degrees now.

As Tomlin glares at me, no doubt trying to figure out why I'm not concentrating and what's causing me to almost drop my child into water that could scald her skin, I shake my head and apologise.

'Sorry,' is all I can mumble and, as Evelyn starts crying, presumably because she is getting cold on account of me having taken all her clothes off in preparation for this bath, Tomlin takes her from me before telling me to put some more cold water in the bath.

I do as he says, not because I'm just blindly following orders but because it is obviously the right thing to do in the situation. As the temperature on the duck goes down, the bath becomes safe for Evelyn to be put into. Once she is in, her crying stops and she looks content sitting there in the shallow water, her eyes on the rubber duck, which is now back to its normal, safe, yellow colour. I don't feel as content as my daughter does because that was just another example of me being a useless mother. Who knows what might have happened if Tomlin hadn't been with me to notice the mistake I was about to make? Hating how useless I seem to be at this parenting thing, I fear, not for the first time, that my past experiences might be to blame for this problem too. The mental and physical toll that Fern's lies have taken on me have left me a shell of my former self. Could it be that my inability to function properly is destroying my chances of being a good mum? I imagine one of the best things a mother can be for their child is present, yet I'm far from that, lost to a million and one worries every single day and unable to focus on the good in my child because I can only see the bad in terms of what that doctor's wife did to me.

I glance at him as he kneels beside me, but he isn't looking at me. He is too busy washing Evelyn and making cooing noises to her, which only makes me feel even more useless because, instead of doing the same, I'm lost to my anxious thoughts once again. That's why I decide to excuse myself from this situation to go and try and clear my head elsewhere, a habit I quickly formed when Evelyn was born because it's the only coping mechanism I seem to have tried that works for at least a short period of time.

Tomlin tells me to go and have a lie down and he will get Evelyn ready for bed. That sounds like music to my ears so I head for the bedroom before collapsing in sheer exhaustion, my head on my soft pillow and my aching body soon covered by the warm duvet. Holding Evelyn so much during the day is wreaking havoc on my back, a part of my body that was already suffering after carrying around such a weight during the latter stages of pregnancy. I suspect I need a chiropractor at some point but first I need a good night's sleep. With Tomlin around to help, I might just get it.

At least that's what I think until I hear his phone ring.

My body turns instantly cold at the sound of the ringtone because I recognise it immediately and I know exactly which phone it is that is ringing. It's not his personal one. It's his work mobile and that can only mean one thing. Sure enough, I am right about that because, as I overhear Tomlin saying that tonight is not a good night and asking if there isn't somebody else who can do it instead, I already know what is coming.

He has been called into work unexpectedly.

That means I'm now going to be left alone with Evelyn.

I hear Tomlin end the call and I know it's only a matter of time until he comes in here and tells me about the conversation he just had with one of his superiors at the police station but, until then, I try to make the most of the final moments of peace I have. My exhausted body does not want to move from this warm, comfortable bed, but it will have no choice soon because, instead of sleeping for five or six hours as I had been hoping, I'm now going to have to be up and down all night, feeding and settling Evelyn. How the hell do single mothers do it? I can't even begin to imagine the day-to-day drain on their mind and bodies, but I do know one thing.

It must be the hardest job in the world.

When Tomlin does appear in the bedroom door with my baby in his arms, he looks as nervous as I feel. The expression on his kind face only makes me feel worse because I can see that he feels uncomfortable about leaving me to look after Evelyn by myself. It's painfully obvious to him that I am struggling, which is why he has been trying to make my life easier by helping so much, but there's not much he can do for me while he's at work.

'I've just been called in,' he says quietly.

'I know. I heard you on the phone.'

'There's been an incident in Carlisle. They need the extra help.'

'Fine. Just go.'

'Are you going to be okay?' Tomlin asks nervously, showing signs of his own fatigue as he runs a hand over his face before stifling a yawn. I've seen him stifle lots of yawns lately and I guess he does that because he feels bad at showing me how tired he is when he knows I must be feeling far worse.

'We'll be fine,' I say before forcing myself out of bed and telling him to give me Evelyn. She's wrapped up inside a towel after her bath and requires changing, feeding and burping before I can even think about trying to get her down for a nap, so that tells me I'm looking at about an hour of work at least before I can lie down myself again. What I'd give to be in my boyfriend's position right now. In a moment, he will get to leave the house, get in his car and drive away and he'll spend the next several hours around other adults doing adult things. Sure, whatever incident he might be on his way to help out with might be a grisly one; he's seen plenty of awful things in his line of work as a detective. Given the choice, I think I'd swap places with him tonight, just out of sheer desperation for a change of scene. But that's not an option, and after handing Evelyn to me Tomlin quickly puts his suit on, one of his many fairly fashion-less looks, and then he is ready to go.

'I'll be back as soon as I can,' he tells me, that nervous look still on his tired face as I catch him watching me getting Evelyn dressed.

'Just go,' I say, wearily repeating what I said to him when he first told me he had been called away, though I'm sure he detects the undertones that I'm not saying it to convince him that I'll be fine, rather that I'm utterly fed up, yet I have no other choice in the matter. Whether he registers that or not, Tomlin leaves the house and the sound of the door closing behind him is the signal that I'm on my own again now.

'Are you going to be a good girl for Mummy tonight?' I ask Evelyn, aware that she can't answer me with real words, but hoping that the sound of my voice might at least illicit a small smile or anything to make me feel like my child appreciates me for all the hard work I am doing. All that happens is Evelyn starts crying and she remains extremely agitated until I am able to put a bottle in her mouth and pump her full of milk. That seems to be the only thing I can ever do to calm her down, but at least she's quiet, and by the time I have finished the feed, she actually looks like she might sleep.

Saying a silent prayer to the gods of parenting, I lower Evelyn into her crib and hope she will not wake up anytime soon. Amazingly, she does seem to be at peace, so I quickly get myself into bed too and then say one more quick prayer, asking for at least a couple of hours sleep until my motherly duties are required again. All I end up getting is fifteen minutes because Evelyn wakes and starts screaming, causing me to hit the mattress beneath me in frustration before letting out a scream of my own.

I wish more than anything that I had the patience to deal with my daughter in a more caring and composed way. Is it this hard for everyone? No matter my personal circumstances and whatever excuses I can make about Fern, the fact remains that all Evelyn wants is for her mother to do a good job of looking after her, yet I'm failing miserably on that front. Then I wish that Tomlin was here so he could step in but he's already several miles away, so I have two choices now. I have to pick Evelyn up and try and soothe her back to sleep myself. Or, I could leave the room, closing the door behind me, and give Evelyn a chance to self-soothe. I could then go downstairs where things are a little quieter and therefore, a little easier. I wouldn't leave her for long, just for enough time so I could calm down and claw back a bit of energy to start the whole process all over again.

I'm sitting in the kitchen two minutes later with the radio on and a glass of wine on the table in front of me. I can still hear Evelyn a little bit, but the music is drowning out most of her cries and, while I feel guilty, the wine does taste good and is about the only thing keeping me from having a meltdown right about now. I'm just going to give her a few minutes to settle, then I'll go and check on her.

Seeking further solace with my phone, I check my messages and, when I do, I'm surprised but pleased to see I have a new one from a friend – the only positive thing that came out of my awful experience in prison.

The name in my inbox is Siobhan, the one inmate I became friendly with behind bars, and things have changed a lot since we both used to spend our days talking together while surrounded by dangerous criminals and overzealous wardens. She was serving a sentence for attempted murder of her former boss but, despite that frightening fact, she was nothing but kind to me and was the one ray of light in that dark place where I languished for so long before justice was served and I was released. Siobhan herself had been released just before me, and since then she has moved back to Ireland where she's attempting to rebuild her life, much like I have been trying to do. We have kept in touch with messages checking in on each other, and she kindly sent me a congratulations card when Evelyn was born. Now it seems Siobhan wants to go one step further to show just how much she still thinks of me as a friend because, after reading her message, I find out that she wants to come and visit me.

She has written that she is coming over to the UK for a short holiday and is wondering whether I might be able to accommodate her for a night or two. I'm more than happy to say yes. Typing out a quick reply, I tell her that it would be wonderful to see her and that she is more than welcome to stay with me for as long as she likes. I briefly consider consulting Tomlin about this because he lives here too now but he's not here currently. I'm also aware that, given her criminal history, Tomlin might not be thrilled about having a woman convicted of attempted murder enter our personal lives. I know Siobhan much better than the police, the prosecutors and the jury can say they do, and she is not just a woman who broke the law once.

She is a friend, and I need all the friends I can get at a time like this.

I send back my message to Siobhan, feeling excited about the prospect of seeing her at some point in the near future. But that's all I'm excited about; as the song on the radio finishes playing, I hear that Evelyn is still crying upstairs.

Damn it, I should go and check on her. Before I do, I wonder if I should check on my boyfriend too. I know he got called to an incident tonight, but I don't know what it is and he might need the encouragement of a friendly message from me to cheer him up. That's why I send him a quick text to tell him that I hope he's okay and that Evelyn and I can't wait until he's home. It's only a small thing, but it's my little way of showing I appreciate him and what he's done for me and my baby recently. It might not seem like it most of the time, particularly to the downtrodden detective, but I am grateful to him. Is that all I am or am I in love with him as well? I'm not sure, though that answer might say it all. Tomlin is reliable, much less unpredictable than Drew was and far more hands-on than Rory, my late husband, who was loyal but had his own flaws as well. But as for pure, pulsating passion and love for my new man? Maybe not, at least not yet anyway. But who has time for feeling a thing like that in the middle of raising a baby?

I feel better for sending him the message but he doesn't reply, no doubt far too busy for that.

However, while he might have his problems tonight, I have plenty of my own problems too. I wearily go upstairs to have another go at soothing Evelyn.

EIGHT

TOMLIN

It's not the late-night drive from Arberness to Carlisle that is bugging me, nor is it the fact that I was supposed to be off work tonight only to receive an unexpected call to come in and assist my colleagues. What's really playing on my mind and causing me to grip this steering wheel a little tighter than is necessary is my anxiety about Alice and her bond with her baby, or rather, *the lack of it*.

As I cruise along this quiet road in the north of England, passing properties where the residents are sleeping soundly inside, I'm hoping Alice and Evelyn are asleep too, although that is unlikely. It's annoying I got called away this evening because it was an opportunity for me to let Alice rest while I looked after the baby, but, as it is, my job has got in the way of that. It's not the first time my professional life has interfered with my personal one, but there aren't many detectives who get to enjoy a work/life balance. There also aren't many detectives who get to keep their jobs after making so many mistakes, so I suppose I should be grateful to still be gainfully employed.

Despite always endeavouring to do the best job I can and proudly representing the police force, I have got things wrong throughout my career. It might not seem like it, considering I've ascended to the position of detective, but I'm not perfect at my job. But is anyone? I'm not the only one who makes mistakes in this line of work but, unfortunately for me, my mistakes have ended up being very high profile, which means these days my reputation often precedes me. Rather than walking into a crime scene and being known as the guy who can crack any case, I'm now known as the guy who spectacularly messed up the biggest investigation this part of the UK has seen for quite some time.

It was bad enough that I helped send an innocent woman to prison, mistakenly falling for Fern's clever plot and finding Alice guilty of Drew's murder. But even when I realised my mistake and tried to rectify it, I have been unable to bring Fern into custody and, as long as she remains at large, I'll always be known as the detective who let her get away on his watch. A case as big as that one could have made my career but instead it has broken it; no longer do I see myself progressing further up the career ladder. I've done well just to keep the job I do have, and while I'm still trying to do it to the best of my ability, the fact that ability has been called into question by members of the public, the media and some of my own colleagues is galling.

Nobody wants to be the detective who got it wrong, but that's me.

With all that has happened before, it's no wonder people were surprised when they found out I was in a relationship with the innocent woman I mistakenly helped send to prison. Ideally, I'd have kept my love life under wraps, but there was little chance of that because there's always been one or two journalists hanging around Arberness looking for a story ever since Fern Devlin turned it into one of the most interesting places for a news scoop. That's how Alice and I ended up being pictured together for the first time as we took Evelyn for a walk along the beach a couple of weeks ago. To say my new romance would come as a surprise to the public and my colleagues would be an understatement, but it was also a surprise to me too because I had never expected to find love with a woman I once helped convict. However, as has become painfully clear to me over the last year or so, life is extremely unpredictable, and who am I to try and second guess it?

My relationship with Alice had been entirely professional – from the first time I met her after Drew's body had been discovered, to the moment she was released from Carlisle prison, my sincerest apologies for getting it wrong ringing in her ears as she made her way back to Arberness to restart her life. Things only started to stray into more personal territory when it had become apparent that Alice was considering suing the police for mistakenly sending her to prison. Nobody wanted that, not just because she clearly had a strong case and it would cost a lot of money, but because it would bring even greater shame on everybody involved in the whole investigation and presumably result in several job losses. That was why I took it upon myself to go and speak to Alice to see if I could convince her to not sue, which was a hard sell and something I probably would have been advised not to do by my superiors, but something I decided to take a chance on, if only to try and reduce the pressure that was already on me and my employers, given how badly we had botched the whole case. The media were already all over us, scathing in their reports, but we didn't need the public disapproval growing as strong, which would happen if it was reported that taxpayers' money had been used to pay off a wrongfully convicted woman.

When I went to see Alice, I found her in the late stages of her pregnancy, cradling her sizeable bump and looking like a woman who was not quite sure whether or not she was ready for what parenthood had in store for her. She was not exactly pleased to see me on her doorstep, which was understandable, but I managed to persuade her to hear what I had to say and, once I did, I did my best to show her that she wasn't the only one hurting over what Fern had done. I was brutally honest with Alice, explaining how there hadn't been a day that had gone by when I hadn't regretted getting it wrong, and that while it was perfectly reasonable for Alice to blame the police, really, there was only one person to blame, and that was the person we were still working on catching. Surprisingly, Alice agreed with me, and she admitted the whole idea of suing the police had been more her lawyer's than her own. She told me that financially she was okay because her husband's life insurance was paying out, plus there was a chance she could end up having some of Drew's life insurance money paid out to her on account of having his child, though that money has been currently on hold ever since Fern had gone on the run. But it was clear she was too busy, too tired or simply too driven by hating the doctor's wife to obsess over the money. She had enough to get by, which allowed her to focus on what she really wanted, and that was Fern.

While Alice had her issues, it was a relief to see that they weren't directed at me and my profession. Rather than finding a woman full of hate for me as a detective and my colleagues, she seemed to be reserving all of her hate for Fern and on that we could find common ground, which may be why things eventually progressed to what they have become now.

It became apparent to me during that meeting that Alice was struggling and anxious about life as an impending single mum. That was when I first started to become more than just the detective who had worked on her case. I offered to help, simply because it seemed like the right thing to do. I said I could go and get groceries for her or complete a couple of the DIY tasks that needed doing around her house. I also offered her the chance to call me, day or night, if she ever had a problem and needed somebody to talk to. I was aware that while she had some friends in Arberness, and a few family members in Manchester, she seemed to mostly be choosing to struggle on by herself. It turned out that such an offer led to numerous late-night phone conversations between us in which, together, we processed our shock, grief and shame over what Fern had done to us both, before also entertaining ourselves with talk of all the delicious ways we would love to get revenge on her.

I was wary of my colleagues discovering my growing relationship with Alice and questioning whether it was particularly professional of me to be getting involved with a woman whose case I had worked on, but despite learning of it and being surprised, they haven't said anything negative towards me. I guess my bosses saw the photos in the newspapers recently, the ones of me and Alice on the beach, but chose to turn a blind eye to it, no doubt just relieved they hadn't been sued like they could have been.

As talks of our revenge intensified, as far as I was concerned, that revenge only extended to wanting to see Fern caught and locked up for her crimes, so I never felt too bad having such conversations. It became clear the more we had them the closer Alice and I were growing. We only grew closer when Alice had Evelyn and, while I wasn't present at the birth, I sent her food parcels, flowers and even more offers of help as I attempted to make her transition into motherhood as easy as possible.

I'll admit that I wasn't being entirely selfless because I was also lonely in my own life, a divorcee who had little to look forward to after arriving home from a day at work. Not to mention I was attracted to Alice. She had always been a woman capable of turning a man's head, her blonde hair and blue eyes clearly having been just a few of her appealing characteristics that led Drew Devlin down his path of self-destruction. I'm also not too stupid to see that Alice was lonely as well, and most likely would never have taken such an interest in me if circumstances had been different in her life. As it was, we were two struggling souls bonded by our shared history with Fern. That was how our relationship started and it's what bonds us together now, although it's not exactly a romantic basis for a couple. For a start, we haven't been physical much. This can mostly be put down to Alice having a baby around the time we got together. Going through such a thing is hardly an aphrodisiac for a woman and I didn't expect her to want to jump straight into bed with me after what her body had been through. I have been hopeful we would be more intimate as time passed, although that's not quite happened yet; Alice is not in the right mental space for anything like that, meaning we're more like house-mates than lovers.

As I drive on, I feel a nagging sense of worry that my relationship with her might not last. There is no doubt that things are strained between us and that strain is caused by how hard she is finding it to take care of Evelyn. Speaking for myself, I am loving my role as a sort of stepfather to the baby girl, and I relish the opportunity to help out with her as much as I can. Having never imagined I'd be a dad, I'm grateful for the opportunity to have an impact on a child's life; there is a big part of me that hopes that Alice and I work out so that, as Evelyn grows, we can be a family. But that remains to be see; these days it feels like all Alice and I do is argue, the sleep deprivation and the commit-ment required for my job meaning things aren't easy.

However, I do have a potential ace up my sleeve. It's one thing that, if I can do it, would surely make Alice want to be with me even more and realise just how much I care for her. It's something that I have been working on secretly, unbeknownst to her and my colleagues in the police force.

I have enlisted the help of an old friend who is currently working to try and find Fern for me.

When most boyfriends are trying to stay in the good graces of their partners, they might simply buy something for them. Flowers. Chocolates. Jewellery. Perhaps a date night. Dinner and a movie. Anything like that can usually work. I'm aware that there is only one thing I can give to Alice at this time that would really cheer her up, and I have had no choice but to pursue it.

Alice is desperate for Fern to be caught, which is why I'm hoping I can give her that present that would trump all else.

My old friend currently on the case for me is an ex-colleague, Ian, who retired as a detective but recently got in touch with me after hearing all about my professional troubles in the news. He offered his sympathy and told me to stay strong, but he also offered something else too.

Help.

Telling me he was bored with life as a retiree and seeking a challenge, he wondered if he could help track down Fern. There was certainly no bigger case facing the police force in this country, both then and now. I thanked him but didn't expect him to actually take to his task so earnestly. However he has and, while he hasn't found Fern yet, he is out there now, working diligently towards doing that. Crucially, he is operating free from the politics and bureaucracy of the police, things that have and continue to hamper my efforts here, and that's why I am hopeful that he will be the first one to have a breakthrough.

I haven't told Alice about Ian because I want it to be a big surprise when, hopefully, we have some good news soon. Until then, all I can do is try and make things as easy as I can for her and Evelyn at home, while also try and hang onto my job that could easily have been taken away from me thanks to that devious, deadly woman.

Where are you, Fern?

We will find you.

It's just a matter of time.

NINE

FERN

The only thing more annoying than listening to the broken tap in my flat dripping away is having to request my landlord, Nigel, come and take a look at it. I'm expecting the unsavoury character at my door any moment now. For that reason, I have made sure to change out of my dressing gown and put on some proper clothes, ones that cover every part of my body, so there is no chance Nigel gets a peek at any bare flesh and gets overexcited. He's already made a couple of passes at me before, not to mention dropped several strong hints that he is single and available. They are passes and suggestions that I promptly rejected because being around that man makes my skin crawl, although what is frightening is that, as the date for my next rental payment approaches, I am struggling to see how I can come up with the full amount. This means Nigel won't just be making inappropriate suggestions about me paying him in some other way soon.

It literally might come down to me having the choice between sleeping with him or being kicked out onto the street and living homeless with Cecilia by my side.

That's all the motivation I need to make sure that doesn't

happen and that is why, as Cecilia is taking a nap in her crib, I am hunched over the second-hand laptop, which I was recently able to buy for a knockdown price, and I'm having another go at trying to crack the password to Drew's offshore account.

Attempting to access my late husband's funds shouldn't be this hard, and it wouldn't be in normal circumstances, but these are far from normal. To emphasise how strange this all is, there is the very real possibility my late husband's life insurance policy, the one I was enjoying the fruits of before I went on the run, may end up being redistributed towards the woman he was cheating on me with. Having had Drew's child, Alice may be entitled to some of the money in order to raise his baby in his absence, and the thought of her spending the money that should have been mine makes me furious. I was with Drew for years, married him, built a life together while she simply swanned in, slept with him several times and then now what? She gets rich off her affair?

What a joke. If I could have predicted the future, I'd have spent every penny of that insurance money so Alice had nothing to access, but none of us have a crystal ball.

Then again, even if I did, I probably wouldn't have believed what it showed me based on what's happened since.

Gritting my teeth, I tell myself to forget about another woman's financial situation and focus on improving my own, and that will be the case if I can use this crummy laptop to get me into Drew's secret bank account. But this laptop was cheap for a reason. A couple of the keys don't work, one is missing and when I hit ENTER, there's a fifty-fifty chance of it actually doing what it's supposed to do. I needed to buy it because I needed some way of being connected to the internet and this was all I could afford. However, time is running out for me to crack this password and soon I might have to sell this laptop back to the shop where I bought it to raise some much-needed funds, so I have to work quickly.

As far as guessing the password goes, I've long ago exhausted all the obvious options. I've entered things like Drew's favourite sports teams, names of childhood pets and any nicknames he might have had or used for me, which resulted in nothing. I've also tried things like his favourite number or colour, but that hasn't got me anywhere either. Most vexingly of all, I have also tried Alice's name, wondering if my late husband could have been using the name of his mistress to secure his online account. That didn't work either, which was relieving and frustrating in equal measure.

He has a password that is tough to guess, which is obviously the whole point of these things, but why couldn't he be the type of idiot who just used their name followed by 123? Even in death, that man is tormenting me and, not for the first time, I'm afraid that I'll never guess the combination of letters and numbers I need to access this account. Without it, I will be screwed financially and not only be left unable to provide a roof over Cecilia's head but without the funds required to even feed her.

It's not just the password to the offshore account I am having a go at hacking. I'm also trying to gain access to Drew's personal email account because I think that, if I can get in there, there is a chance I can click the 'Forgot Password' button on his bank account and may be able to set up a new one. I'm no nearer to getting into his emails either, but it only takes one look at the peaceful young girl sleeping soundly beside me to force me to keep on trying.

Think, Fern, think. What else can I try that I haven't already?

With renewed hope, I enter the name of one of the characters in his favourite TV show, followed by his lucky number, but that doesn't work. Then I try a few of Drew's favourite authors, but again, nothing. If there's one positive in my so far fruitless quest to crack this code, it's that his email account doesn't have one of those systems that only allows for a certain number of guesses before the user is locked out. That gives me the opportunity to keep on guessing, though that's not getting me anywhere yet. However, it's a different story for his bank account as, on there, I only get five attempts in any twenty-four-hour period, so I have to be far more selective with what I try there. It's also why I'm aware this could take me a lot longer yet.

Annoyingly, a moment later, I hear movement at my front door and I know I'm going to have to pause what I am doing because I'm about to have company.

Closing my laptop so that my landlord won't be able to take a sneak peek at what I was doing, I get up and go to the door, conscious that he's more likely to try and take a sneak peek at my curves than anything on my computer screen. But I don't even make it to the door before it opens, Nigel clearly deciding that he would rather use the key he has to this place than knock politely and allow me to answer the door in my own home. Technically, he does own this flat, but I don't appreciate him just walking in and I make sure to let him know it. He apologises, but judging by the look on his face, he's less sorry for barging in and sorrier because he has just realised that he hasn't caught me in some state of undress.

'How's the tap?' he asks me, the disappointment evident on his face as he eyes up my baggy jumper and tracksuit bottoms, possibly wondering why I couldn't have made a bit more of an effort for his visit today.

'Still leaking,' I say, and I allow him to take a look at it while I go back to Cecilia and take a seat beside her, subconsciously feeling like I have to be a little more protective of my little one now there is a man in this flat with us. Or maybe I'm just trying to remind Nigel that I've recently had a baby and, as such, any thoughts of sexual advances towards me should be the furthest thing from his mind.

'Sounds like you need a knight in shining armour,' Nigel

says as he leans over the sink to examine the tap. He doesn't see me roll my eyes at him, unimpressed with the idea of him coming to my rescue.

'Is it going to take long to fix? I've got some work to do,' I say, hoping to speed this up, but Nigel either doesn't hear me or ignores me completely.

'How's things? You must get bored being here all day with just the little one for company,' Nigel says, and he looks back at me with a suggestive smile on his face.

'I'm fine,' I reply before enquiring about the tap again.

'Hmm, I'm going to need to order a new one, I think,' comes the response I didn't want to hear.

'You can't fix it now? It's keeping me awake at night.'

'The tap or the baby?'

The answer to that is both, but I don't say it.

'I'll be back with a new one soon,' Nigel tells me.

'How soon?'

'I don't know. A day or two.'

'Can't you do it quicker?'

'Depends how motivated I am,' Nigel says, and that suggestive smile is back again, which makes my stomach churn.

'A day or two is fine,' I quickly reply, shutting that train of conversation down instantly.

As Nigel checks under the sink, I put a hand on Cecilia's chest as she begins to stir from her latest nap, and I wonder if the window of opportunity for me to guess the password is closing again for the time being, because I might have to be on mummy duties for the next hour or so. But her eyes stay closed as Nigel finishes up at the sink; he asks me if there is anything else he can do for me while he is here, a question that did not need the wink that accompanied it. I tell him I'm fine and show him out.

I relax a little when he's gone but only slightly because I know he'll be back soon to fix the tap, just like I know he will soon be demanding his rent payment and currently I don't have it. That's why I quickly open the laptop again and get back to work.

Alternating between the bank account and the email account, I try several more combinations and nothing is working until I think of a name I haven't tried yet. It's a name that means something to Drew but it means something to me too, which is why I feel a shiver run down my spine as I consider it.

Roger.

That's the name of Drew's favourite tennis player, as in Roger Federer, and I think how it is worth a shot to try it as his password. But that name also reminds me of the man who tricked me after Drew's death. Greg, posing under the fake name Roger, was a friend of Drew's. He pretended to be my boyfriend to find out the truth about Drew's murder and almost exposed my lies until I killed him. The last thing I needed was a flashback to that hotel room when I stabbed him to death with a broken beer bottle, but that's what I've got right now. However, I have not tried that name as a password yet, so I quickly change that.

RogerFederer – incorrect password.

Federer123 – incorrect password.

Roger123 – incorrect password.

Rogerfan123 – incorrect password.

Federerfan123...

I can't believe it! I'm in! Okay, so it's only Drew's email account, but I quickly go over to his bank account to try the same password, hoping that it works there too. Sadly, it does not, but at least with access to his old emails I can request a reset password link now, and that's exactly what I plan to do. Just before I get to that, my eyes flit over some of the subject headings of the emails in my late husband's inbox and that's how I see a name I recognise.

Alice.

In amongst a few generic newsletter emails from some of the places Drew used to frequent, like the tennis club he played at or a restaurant he occasionally received discount offers from, I see the name of his mistress sitting right here in his inbox too. By the looks of it, Drew received an email from Alice only yesterday, which seems strange because why would she be emailing a dead person?

There's only one way to find out so I open the email and, when I do, I see the short but unsweet message she sent to the deceased doctor.

I hate you!

That's it. That's all the email says. Why would Alice send such a thing, knowing Drew was never going to see it? Unless she was just having a moment where her hatred for that man overrode any kind of sensible thought. Wow, she really must mean it. But she's not the only one; I hate Drew too, although seeing that Alice feels exactly the same way is a bit of a surprise. I often imagined she'd be mourning the man she was having an affair with, wishing things had turned out differently and that he was still alive so she could be continuing to have all sorts of illicit fun with him. I guess not, and seeing an email such as this one makes me think Alice's life is not going well at all. I mean, a happy person does not send aggressive emails to a dead man, do they?

Particularly at three o'clock in the morning.

Curious as to what other kind of possible correspondence might be present in this inbox, I do a search for her name to see how many other emails were sent between her and my husband. When I do that, I get a couple of results back, specifically, two emails that were sent when my husband was still alive.

I clock the first one and see that it was an email from Drew to Alice. In it, he apologises for getting in touch with her but goes on to say that he just wants to speak to her and figured this was the best way rather than messaging her phone because her husband might see it. It's clear from the tone of the message that Drew is eager to extract a response from Alice because he is asking for her to give him another chance. This is surprising because, by the sounds of it, he is desperate to see her, but she might not be quite as desperate to see him. I get confirmation of that when I click the next message and see that Alice replied and told him that she meant what she said about them needing to stop seeing each other and that she doesn't think it's fair on either of their partners to be doing what they have been doing behind our backs.

I'm stunned by what I'm reading because, despite always having in my mind the image of Alice being a homewrecker who never thought of anybody but herself, I'm seeing a very different side of her here.

Does that change how I think of her?

I'm not sure I'd go that far, but it's clear from this very short correspondence that Drew was the one actively pursuing her. I suppose that fits in perfectly with what he did next. By looking at the dates of these emails, I can see that they were sent before he suggested the pair of us move to Arberness, and that move was all about him trying to get closer to his mistress again. I had figured Alice had tried to end things when she moved away from Manchester, thus putting her affair on ice, but I can see clearly here that, even before that, she was having reservations about it.

Maybe I have been too harsh on her.

Drew deserved what I did to him, but did Alice?

No good can come from me suddenly having a crisis of confidence about any revenge I've undertaken in the past, so I close the emails and decide not to look at them anymore. I need to focus on the future, not the past, and that is why I don't waste any more time. I navigate my way back to the website for

Drew's offshore account and click the 'Forgot Password' button. It offers to send me a link to reset it, which I have no problem doing now that I have full access to Drew's email account and, a moment later, I am creating new log in credentials. A moment after that, I try them out for the first time before holding my breath to see if it works.

It does.

I'm in.

But far from thinking that some of my problems might be about to be solved, I realise something.

Maybe, they are only just beginning.

TEN

ALICE

Last night was hard work, with no sleep and no boyfriend around to help me with Evelyn. I'm still waiting for Tomlin to get home from work. He's been gone for over twelve hours, and while he sent me a text this morning asking how I was, that's all I've heard from him. Things must be busy at the police station but they're busy here too. As I finish yet another feed, I'm desperate to get out of the house and get some fresh air. But while I did have hopes of putting Evelyn in her pram and taking her for a walk, the weather has had other ideas and I don't fancy taking her out in the rain. She'd get cold and wet and that would only give her another reason to cry, not that she seems to need any more of them. She's bawling again, her face bright red and small teardrops resting on the ends of her tiny eyelashes, and despite trying to calm her down by holding and rocking her, as always, it doesn't work.

The only thing that has been getting me through the day so far has been caffeine, but even that is no longer strong enough. After putting Evelyn down for a moment, I pour myself a glass of wine and take a hearty gulp. After I've done that, I check my messages again to see if Siobhan has replied and she has, telling me that while she doesn't have an exact date when she will be over to visit me yet, it will be soon and she will let me know when her plans are worked out. I reply to tell her that is absolutely fine, and it is, because whenever she can come and see me sounds good to me. No sooner will I have introduced her to Evelyn than I will be taking Siobhan into the village where we will be spending a very long night at the pub while Tomlin babysits. It's just what I need.

An adult activity.

Bliss.

Until then, I'm stuck with drinking alone with only a crying baby for company, but after two glasses, I hear a car parking outside. Going to the window, I see that Tomlin is finally back from work and, while he looks tired himself, he probably knows better than to walk through the door and say how sleepy he is considering that I've been busy too while he's been gone.

We've been snapping at each other a bit lately, so I decide to make more of an effort with him when he gets in to try and keep the peace, for all our sakes. Maybe my mood is improved by the wine I have consumed but, whatever it is, I put a big smile on my face as he walks in before asking him how his latest shift was.

'Gruelling,' comes the weary response before Tomlin approaches me and gives me a kiss on the cheek. That's about as physical as the two of us ever get but it's nice, or at least I think it is until he pulls back with a concerned look on his face.

'Have you been drinking?' he asks me and, suddenly, despite me hoping that things would get easier when he was home, it seems they might just be about to get worse.

'I had one glass of wine,' I say with a shrug, to make out like it is no big deal and maybe it wouldn't be, except it wasn't just one I had. Tomlin can see that because there isn't much left in the wine bottle sitting on the table beside my glass.

'What are you doing? It's the middle of the day!' Tomlin

cries, exasperated. 'And you shouldn't be drinking while you're alone with Evelyn. What if you had to drive her somewhere?'

'Where?'

'I don't know. The doctor's? The hospital? You should be sober.'

'I am sober!'

'Are you?'

'Yes!'

'What if you'd fallen asleep? Do you know how many instances I've heard of in my career where a parent has passed out drunk with their baby and something terrible has happened?'

'Oh, stop overreacting. It was just one or two glasses of wine. I'm still perfectly capable of looking after my baby.'

Despite me saying that and meaning it, he does not look convinced, which hurts; nobody wants their abilities as a guardian called into question. To prove him wrong, I go to pick up Evelyn, though when I do, she cries even louder and does little to aid my argument.

'How long has she been crying for?' Tomlin asks me as he moves in to help.

'She never stops!' I reply before deciding it's just easier to hand her over to him than stand here and try and make a point.

As he attempts to calm my baby down, I decide to tell him about the news I have, if only to change the subject from us talking about how much of a bad parent I might be.

'I have a friend who is going to be coming to stay,' I tell him breezily, hoping he'll just say that sounds good and not ask for any details.

'Who?'

No such luck.

'Siobhan.'

Tomlin frowns.

'Who's that?'

'My friend from prison,' I reply, wishing there was a way I could have said that breezily but there isn't and, once again, Tomlin is frowning at me.

'Your friend from prison?'

'Yeah, is there a problem?'

There clearly is, but I'm at least pretending like there shouldn't be.

'What was she in prison for?'

'It doesn't matter. She's out now and is trying to get on with her life, just like I am.'

'Don't pretend like you're the same. You were innocent, she wasn't. There's a huge difference.'

I didn't need him to spell that out for me and I shake my head to show just how much I don't appreciate it.

'She was a good friend to me while I was on the inside and it will be nice to see her.'

'What was she in prison for?' he asks again, disdain in his voice and evident on his face.

'Attempted murder,' I reply, and no sooner have I said those words than I know they aren't going to help me persuade him that having such a person in our home is a good idea.

'Are you insane? In what world do you think it's smart to have an attempted murderer coming to visit where your baby is?'

'She tried to kill her old boss, not steal a child!' I cry, defending her. 'And she's a good person. She just made a mistake.'

'She's a convicted criminal, and clearly a dangerous one at that!'

'Not everybody who goes to prison is a bad person. You should know that better than anyone. You sent me there, remember, and I was innocent!'

That was a low blow, but I've said it now and there's no denying it has helped me in this argument; it has shut Tomlin up. There isn't much he can say to something like that because I only said the truth.

Evelyn's crying is getting louder and, presumably, she is picking up on all the stress going on around her, which tells both of us that we need to stop arguing. That's easier said than done because we're both tired and mad at each other, so we need a break. Seeing as I've been here with the baby for so long, I decide the person getting the break ought to be me and grab my coat before heading for the door.

'Where are you going?' Tomlin asks me, sounding surprised that I'd leave at a time like this.

'We need milk and nappies!' I say, which is partly true, but is not the only reason I'm going out. I just need any excuse to leave this house for a short time and, as I step outside, I don't feel bad for going. Nor do I feel bad when, instead of heading in the direction of the village shop, I go towards the beach. At a time like this and as stressed as I am, I feel like I need to be by the water, so I keep going until the Solway Firth comes into view.

Gazing across the sea and sand, I get a glimpse of Scotland in the distance, but the view is still not quite enough to calm me down yet, so I keep walking and, the further I go, the closer I get to two places that are notable for all the wrong reasons.

The first is one of the houses that overlooks this picturesque place. I can see the impressive property that Fern and Drew moved into when they arrived in Arberness. Like every other local resident here, we were all slightly envious of whichever couple it would be who got to move into the large and expensive home that had gone up for sale. It was quite the shock when I realised exactly who it was; having Drew follow me here and buy this house was just a strong example of how desperate he was to rekindle the affair I had put a stop to in Manchester.

As I walk past the impressive house, I glance at the front window and, when I do, I see another couple inside, sitting on their sofa and watching the television. They don't notice me, nor do they have any idea that I have been inside their home before, back when I was invited to a dinner party that Fern was hosting. I attended with my late husband Rory and the idea was that it was a double date with Fern and Drew, but, in hindsight, I now know that Fern knew all about my affair with her husband and was simply playing games with the pair of us, putting us into an awkward situation and watching the pair of us squirm across the dinner table from each other.

I wonder if the couple who live in this house these days know the full history of the place they now call home. Possibly, because it did make national news, but even if they did know this house was once the home of the doctor who died and the wife who plotted to kill him, it clearly didn't put them off making an offer and moving their things in once that offer was accepted. Or maybe they got the place at a heavily reduced rate, taking advantage of the fact the previous owners had been so infamous, and helping out whichever unlucky estate agent had been tasked with trying to sell it. It's funny, but even if a house has a horrible history, some people don't care, prioritising the extra space and prestigious postcode over anything that might have happened with the previous owners. I suppose nobody actually died in that house, so it's not too bad.

That's because it was on the beach where the previous man of the house lost his life.

As I head down onto the sand, the wind picks up around me, perhaps a sign from the weather gods that I should turn back and go home rather than carry on to the place I'm heading towards. Nothing good can surely come of me going to a certain part of this beach, yet I'm going there anyway, undeterred, perhaps foolishly so.

As I get nearer to the specific spot on the sand, I think about what it must have been like here on that fateful night. Even windier than this, I imagine. Colder too because it was mid-winter. And quiet. Oh, so very quiet. At least until the murder weapon made contact with a skull, anyway.

I stop walking when I reach my destination and look around me. But all I see are grains of sand and they are the colour they should be. There are no red specks – signs of blood that shouldn't be here because those washed away months ago. But they were here before.

That's because this is the exact part of the beach where Drew Devlin met his maker.

As I predicted, nothing good is coming from me being here, but I linger for too long, my head filling with all sorts of nasty images of Fern, Rory and Drew down at this beach and saying whatever things were said between them before the doctor perished. My ex-husband went home to me and Fern went back to her house and waited for the police to discover the grisly scene. I wonder what was said that night. Best not to know. Maybe I'll find out one day if Fern is ever caught. Right now, that feels about as likely as me counting exactly how many grains of sand there are on this beach.

Standing in the spot where Drew died, I think about the email I sent to him in the early hours of this morning. Tired, angry and utterly fed up with my screaming baby, I fired off an unnecessary message to the late doctor's inbox, one that nobody will ever get to read, but one I felt like sending anyway. I told him that I hated him and, while it was completely pointless, I did feel slightly better for all of five seconds because it was the most I could do to vent my frustration at the man who followed me here, restarted our affair and, ultimately, caused my life to end up like it has.

Upsettingly, my hatred of Drew is possibly another reason I am struggling to bond with my baby. She's his as well as mine, which means there will always be a part of her father inside her and, when I look at her, I think of him. That's not Evelyn's fault; no baby chooses who their parents are or what they might have done before they were born. But it is a fact.

My daughter's father is the man who has made my life so hard.

The sound of my phone ringing brings me back into the present and, when I take it out of my coat pocket, I see that it is Tomlin who is calling me. He's probably checking where I am because I should have been back from the supermarket by now, which is a problem, because I've not even gone there yet. I consider not answering, but that will only annoy him even more, so I connect the call. But when I do, I don't hear Tomlin asking me where I am or telling me that Evelyn needs her mum. Instead, what he has to say sounds much more promising.

'Come home, I've got some news,' he tells me, and it's impossible to miss how much excitement there is in his voice. What's got my boyfriend so fired up?

'What are you talking about? What news?' I ask him as the wind blows strongly around me again.

'I'll tell you when you get back.'

'Why can't you tell me now?'

'Because I want to see your face when I tell you.'

'What are you talking about?'

There is a pause at the other end of the line.

'I suppose it doesn't matter. I might as well tell you. Guess what? I think I might have found her.'

'Who?'

'Who do you think? Fern!'

'What?'

Of all the things I had been expecting Tomlin to say to me, that was the last one. In fact, it wasn't even on my radar. If anyone was going to find Fern, I thought it would be me. But he's done it? He's achieved the impossible? If so, it's a miracle. It sure feels like one.

'I know where she is,' Tomlin confirms, which is music to my ears and all I need to hear before I'm running across the sand.

I've never been so keen to get home in all my life.

ELEVEN
TOMLIN

It's always nice to deliver good news, especially to a person you care so strongly about and particularly after our last exchange was an argument. While Alice might have been feeling irritated with me when she left the house, there is no doubt she is going to be feeling a whole lot differently towards me when she gets back after what I have just told her.

I wasn't lying when I said I had good news.

Never mind making her day; *I think I've just made Alice's year*.

I can't wait for her to get back, but the time it is taking her suggests she has gone a little further than the local supermarket. I could have guessed that anyway, because it was obvious when she left the house that she was keen to get away and was in no rush to return, though I suspect her legs are carrying her as fast as they can now.

It was a surprise to receive a call from Ian, the ex-detective who I have been keeping busy in retirement by putting him on Fern's trail. Usually, I'm the one calling him, seeking an update and often I end the conversation disappointed because not much is ever forthcoming. I always knew it was never Ian's fault that he had no news, it was just that Fern was too good at hiding. But he had news for me today and, as I finally hear the front door fly open, I'm excited to share it.

'What is it? Has she been arrested?' Alice asks me as she bursts into the room where I am cradling Evelyn. I can see the hope and angst etched all over her face, making it even more obvious just how much she has been living in desperate need of a development like this.

'Not yet,' I say, which already sounds more like bad news than good. 'But we have the name she is currently living under.'

'What?'

'Teresa Brown. That's who Fern is pretending to be and, because we know that, it will make finding her a whole lot easier. All we need to do is look for any women under that name.'

Alice stares at me for a second and I can't help but smile as she does; it's brilliant to see her beautiful brain getting to process something a little more exciting than calculating how many hours of sleep she missed out on last night.

'What? Teresa Brown? How...?'

'How do I know that's her name now? Because I've been paying an old friend to look for her for us and he's good.'

Alice looks even more surprised that I've just told her I was paying somebody to find Fern, but I just nod my head to show that I'm serious.

'I know how important it is to you that we find her, so I've been doing everything I can, both at work and outside of work to try and speed that up. I love you, Alice, and I just want you to get closure.'

It's a relief when Alice seems more touched than annoyed that I have been keeping a secret from her. I take the light in her eyes as a positive sign to carry on explaining.

'Ian has been looking into all sorts of things for me and, because London is one of the last places where Fern was picked up on CCTV, he has been focusing a lot of his efforts there. But up until today, he hadn't found any trace of her. That was until he heard about the arrest of a man in the city who had been selling fake forms of ID.'

'Fake ID?'

'Yes. It's been obvious to everybody that the only way Fern has been able to successfully evade us for all this time is because she must be living under a new identity. That's why, when he heard about this counterfeiter, some guy called Dmitri, from a contact in the London Met, Ian was able to get five minutes with him. He spun some story to his friend there about this suspect possibly being linked to an old case he had worked on, and his friend did him a favour. But really, all Ian wanted to do was ask the suspect if he had provided fake documents to anybody matching Fern's description.'

'And?'

'Dmitri was obviously pretty noncompliant at first, refusing to answer much of anything. It seems his defence is claiming that he was simply visiting the flat where all the fake documents were found during the police raid and that it is his cousin who was the one who was making and selling them all.'

'That's probably a lie.'

'Oh, it's definitely a lie. Dmitri is guilty as sin. But Ian told him that he didn't care about any of that. All he cared about was if Dmitri had been in contact with Fern. He showed him a photo and said she might have changed her appearance, but it didn't matter because no sooner had Ian shown him the photo than Dmitri's eyes had lit up.'

'He recognised her?'

'Yes, he did. And then, after Ian had spun him some story about potentially getting Dmitri a lesser sentence if he told the truth, Dmitri admitted that he had seen Fern in the flat and he had made her several fake documents for her new identity. It turns out that he was actually quite happy to give her up because from what he told Ian, Fern had attacked him and stolen from him.'

'What?'

'Yeah. It seems she hadn't been able to pay the required sum for the fake ID but had managed to get away with it all anyway. Dmitri planned on tracking her down in the future because he knew what name she was living under, but he's obviously left it too late because it sounds like he'll be in prison for a while now. But that's good news for us because now we know she is living under the alias Teresa Brown.'

'Oh my God!' Alice cries. 'So where is she now?'

'That's the thing,' I say, trying to keep my excitement from bubbling over like my partner's already is. 'We don't have her yet, but now we have the name she goes by, all we have to do is look for people registered under that name. Bank accounts. Employment databases. Doctor's patient lists. It's only a matter of time until we find where she is hiding.'

'So the police are looking for her as we speak?'

I pause then because it's the first time Alice has asked me a question that has a slightly tricky answer.

'Not quite. So far, Ian has only told me about this development. He called me as soon as he had finished talking to Dmitri. Said I should hear it first, seeing as I was the detective who worked on the original case with Fern and all. But he is planning on telling the officers in the Met, and when he does, a nationwide manhunt will begin. Isn't that great?'

I can't see how that is anything but great, although Alice suddenly stops smiling and seems to have a reason for not jumping for joy like I thought she might be right about now.

'I want to be the one who finds her,' she says stoically, as if a deep sense of calm has just come over her after such a hectic time.

'What?'

'What if we hold off on telling the police about this and

track her down ourselves?' she suggests. 'Wouldn't that be even better? I get to see her face when she's caught and you get to be the detective who puts her in handcuffs, making up for what happened in the past. It's perfect!'

'I don't understand. We can just have the police look for her. They'll be quicker. There's far more of them than us.'

'But Ian has the name so he can find her, right? There can't be too many Teresa Browns out there who match Fern's age and description. All he has to do is look for one who seems to have moved to a new area. We can find her with his help, and we can bring her in!'

Alice clearly thinks this is the way to go, but I'm not convinced.

'It's far too risky,' I remind the overzealous woman standing before me. 'The more time we leave, the more chance there is for Fern to get away again. She might hear about Dmitri's arrest on the news and realise her cover could be blown.'

'No, she won't. We'll find her first!'

'Then there's the fact she is a murderer,' I go on. 'It's way too dangerous for us to approach her even if we do find her. She's killed before to get away and she'll do the same again if we back her into a corner. I'm not taking the chance of you getting hurt, especially not now we have Evelyn to think about.'

'I can handle her,' Alice says defiantly, but I bet that's exactly what Drew, Rory and Greg thought before she gained the upper hand and left them for dead.

'No way. Not a chance. We're leaving this one to the police.'

'The same police who let her get away the first time?' Alice cries. 'Don't give her that opportunity again! We know Fern better than anybody else. We can do this. We can be the ones to bring her in!'

Alice might make a good point about the police already having had their chance at capturing Fern, and that didn't end so well. I know because I was the one leading them at that time.

Mistakes were made, but they won't be made again. Will they? On the off chance they might be, doesn't Alice deserve to be the one to try and bring this matter to a close? If she did so, it sure would go a long way to alleviating the guilt I feel about the part I played in her misfortune.

'Please,' Alice says as she steps nearer to me and, as she puts her hand on my arm, I feel powerless to deny the wishes of this beautiful, persuasive woman. There's a reason Drew fell for her charms and took such a risk in his marriage, and it's the same reason Greg was willing to risk his life to get close to Fern in order to save Alice from a life in prison. It's because Alice is the kind of woman who can make a man do crazy things.

That's my only explanation for the crazy thing I end up doing then.

I give in and tell Alice that we'll hold off on giving this new information to the police so that we can look for her ourselves. With Ian's continued assistance, we'll track her down and confront her wherever we find her to be hiding. But I don't concede without asking for something myself.

'If I agree to this, you have to do something for me,' I say. 'Not just for me but for Evelyn too. You have to go and speak to somebody about how you're feeling. A doctor, I mean. You know you're struggling and that's perfectly understandable, but I hate seeing you this way and I want you to get help. Promise me you will?'

I swallow hard then, my mouth dry, a symptom of the anxiety I feel after asking such a question.

Alice doesn't look quite as keen to agree to that course of action as the one she suggested, but if it's a choice between her getting the chance to find Fern or someone else doing it, she is always going to take it.

'Fine. I'll go and talk to somebody tomorrow,' she tells me and I'm happy enough with that answer, so I tell her that I'll call Ian and give him his new set of instructions. He might not like them, but I'm sure he'll like the extra money I will offer him to do things our way.

As I hand Evelyn back to her smiling mummy, I take out my phone to make my call to my old friend Ian down in London; I'm ready to tell him that he is to keep this name Teresa Brown to himself for the time being and look for her without any outside help. Then, when he thinks he has her, he is to call me again and we will come to assist.

Maybe Alice is right. Maybe we do know Fern best and maybe we do have the best chance of bringing her in.

Despite agreeing to this very risky plan, I know I am right too.

Fern is dangerous.

But the question is, how dangerous?

It seems we're just about to put that to the test again.

TWELVE

FERN

While it was exciting to see that I had gained access to my late husband's offshore bank account, it wasn't quite so exciting when I realised that accessing the money wasn't going to be as simple as I first thought.

I had presumed, perhaps rather naively, that if I had access to the account, I could simply change the bank details on it and have whatever money was in there transferred to my new account under my fake name. After all, surely by demonstrating that I knew the correct password, it showed I had a right to look at the account, and if anybody ever checked they would probably just assume it had been Drew himself who had logged in and done it. With this bank being based overseas, I doubt they have any clue that the holder of the account has passed away, because I certainly haven't told them as his wife and nobody else knows about this money. But I've had the sudden thought that if anybody ever did check this, or if anybody is actually secretly watching this account right now, then sending the money to an account under the name of Teresa Brown might completely give away the fake identity I have been working so hard to keep concealed. I don't want to have to waste money buying myself a new identity, I'd prefer to keep my current one intact if I can.

With that in mind, maybe it's too risky to transfer this money out under my new name. If so, that's an incredible shame because I'm staring at the numbers on my screen and thinking about all the things I could do with the funds that are just sitting there, waiting to be spent.

There's over £20,000 in this account.

Imagine what I could do with that money.

As I look around my depressing surroundings, I know the first thing I would do would be leave this tiny flat and find myself somewhere better to live. I could put down a small deposit on a house or at least a better flat, one that isn't leased by such a dodgy landlord as the one I have currently. I'm in desperate need of more space and Cecilia is only going to get bigger, so an extra couple of rooms for all her stuff would be a godsend. I know I still won't be able to afford anything like the kind of properties I was accustomed to residing in, but I can upgrade on my current living situation. This money would give us the chance to move to a safer area and that's at the top of my priorities, because who doesn't want to raise their child in the best possible environment? The extra cash would also take the pressure off me when I go to buy food or pay bills and it would mean I could put finding a job on the backburner for a little bit, at least until my daughter is a bit older. More money would also mean that if I did need to, I could put Cecilia into nursery for a day or two a week and I could afford it, which would give me the opportunity to work or simply have a break. It would also be nice for her to socialise with other kids, rather than be stuck at home all day with me in some pokey place that smells of damp.

The sound of the still-dripping kitchen tap to my left only motivates me further to access these funds and buy my way out of this place, so I start thinking hard.

How can I withdraw this money without the transaction ever being traced back to me?

After giving it some thought, I consider setting up another bank account and moving the money there. Although that will take more time, more paperwork, more chances for my false identity to be exposed. There has to be something else, something quicker, and, preferably, something that doesn't involve me having to provide my fake IDs to stern-looking bank employees.

Then I have it. There is only one option I can come up with. I need to use somebody else's bank account to move the funds into. That way, the bank account won't be linked to me, so if the police ever get on the trail and follow the money, it won't lead them to me and my new identity.

Okay, so I need a person to help me. Somebody who I could pay a little bit of this money, who would act as a sort of middleman.

It would have to be somebody I trust. A friend, ideally.

But who?

In my situation, the only person I have is the sleeping baby beside me and, while she is cute and probably loves me, she isn't quite at the stage where she owns a bank account and can withdraw cash for me. I could set up an account in her name, but I'd essentially be the one running it, meaning I'd still be the one linked to the account.

Who else is there?

The knock at my door interrupts that thought, and I automatically go to answer it, expecting it to be Nigel's plumber coming to fix that tap. I pause before opening because there is always a chance it could be the police having found me and come to arrest me. That's why I glance nervously at the bag that sits at the bottom of my bed. It's one I always keep packed in case I need to grab it and make a swift exit out of here with Cecilia. In the event of having to make an emergency exit, I'd go out the back entrance; that route allows me to disappear down the back alleyway and be out onto the main road beyond that. Of course, if the police really had found me then they might already have those exit routes covered and I'd be surrounded, but at least I might stand a chance. Certainly more of a chance than just going out the front way, that's for sure.

But as I peer through the peephole on my door and pray that I won't see a man in uniform staring back at me with hand-cuffs dangling in front of his face, I relax because there's nothing to worry about.

'Oh, hey Victoria,' I say after I unlock my door and greet the smiling woman on my doorstep. 'Are you okay?'

'Yeah, just thought I'd come around for a chat. Do you fancy a cup of tea? I've got some teabags at mine if you don't have any.'

It's a nice idea and, to be honest, I could do with the break from stressing over what to do with Drew's money, so I confirm that I do have teabags and invite my friend in. No sooner has she entered than she is at Cecilia's crib, leaning over it and beaming down at the sleeping angel that rests inside.

'Aww, she's gorgeous,' Victoria whispers so as not to wake her, and I smile before putting the kettle on and getting two cups out of the cupboard. It's lucky that nobody else has come for tea because two cups are all I have, to go with the two plates and the two sets of cutlery and, even then, on most days, I don't need that much.

I think it'll be a long time before I'll be hosting a dinner party again.

'What have you been up to?' Victoria asks me as she takes a seat in my armchair and looks around the cramped interior of my home. At least I know she isn't judging me and how I live because her place looks exactly like this one, minus a few packets of nappies, of course.

'Oh, not much,' I reply as I make the tea. I can hardly say

that I've just cracked the password to my dead husband's secret
bank account and now I'm trying to come up with the best way
to funnel those funds out of it. And then I drop my teaspoon
because I suddenly realise that the answer to my problems
might be right here with me in this flat.

As I look over at Victoria sitting in the armchair and smiling
at the sleeping Cecilia, I wonder if she could help me with my
tricky dilemma. I need somebody else's account to transfer the
money into so I don't give away my new name should the
records ever be accessed in future.

What if that person was Victoria?

The more I think about it, the more I see her as a viable
option. For a start, she's the only friend I have in the world;
none of my old ones can ever hear from me again. Perhaps even
more interestingly, she is just as stuck for money as I am, so
she'll surely be receptive to the idea that I could give her some
cash if she does me a favour. Most of all, I know she loves
Cecilia, so I don't have to worry about her doing anything
stupid like getting suspicious of me and reporting me to the
police. She'll just want to try and help out the baby she adores
and that baby's mother.

Of course, I don't have to admit to Victoria who I am and
exactly why I need this favour doing. There's no way I want to
risk giving her my real name and telling her that the bank
account we are dealing with belongs to the man I plotted to
murder. She doesn't need to know any of that. I can just make
up a cover story. I'm usually pretty good at that sort of thing. I
could just tell her that the account belongs to a relative of mine
who passed away and there's been issues getting the will sorted
so this is the only way I can do it. At least I can if she doesn't see
any bank statements with Drew's name on them, but I'll tell her
not to bother getting a statement, just the cash. I could also drop
some heavy hints about my need to remain largely anonymous
in this because maybe there is an abusive ex-boyfriend in my

past who is looking for me and I can't let him find me or my baby.

A story like that is hardly original in a place like this; I imagine these flats are full of people with complicated life stories who fled their original home and are lying low in a new place, desperate to avoid ever coming into contact with someone or something from their troubled past again. Victoria herself has such a sorry story to tell because, while I never asked her directly when I first met her, she did offer up an insight into her past one day and it was a sad one at that.

The victim of a string of bad relationships, Victoria had often been on the move, restarting her life in various new places before inevitably meeting another man who was not good for her and having to leave when things got too tough. She told me her last boyfriend, a real charmer by the name of Darren, had a problem with alcohol and would often take his bad mood out on her whenever he got back from the pub. She fought back once but quickly realised it wasn't worth it so, one night, while he was passed out on the living room sofa, she packed her things and left. Cornwall was her next stop. She's been here ever since and, so far, she seems happy enough, probably because she has avoided getting close to any of the local males who might only make her life more difficult instead of easier. On top of all that, I suspect Victoria comes from a broken home. I enquired about her family once but she just shut that down quickly, telling me that she has no idea where her father is and she really doesn't want her mother to know where she is.

It was hard not to feel sorry for Victoria and it was even harder not to like her when I saw how good she was with Cecilia. I figured I'd be her friend for as long as either one of us lived around here. But maybe we can both be more than friends to each other.

Maybe we can actually help each other.

'Are you okay?' Victoria suddenly asks me and, when I look

at her, I realise she is staring at me with a concerned look on her face.

'Me? Yeah, I'm fine.'

'I've been talking to you for the last minute, and I don't think you've heard a word I've said,' Victoria explains. I realise then I have been totally lost in my daydream and have missed all of what she has been saying.

'Oh, I'm sorry. I was just thinking about something,' I say as I carry our two teas over.

'Anything I can help with?' Victoria asks me as she gratefully accepts her hot drink and takes a sip while I take a seat on the edge of my bed opposite her.

'Maybe you can,' I say with a smile. 'Let's find out.'

THIRTEEN

ALICE

The adrenaline boost I got from hearing that Fern's new identity had been uncovered has not worn off yet, even though it's been twenty-four hours since Tomlin first told me what was happening.

It was a huge surprise to discover my boyfriend had been secretly working to try and catch Fern, not just for the sake of his reputation but for the sake of me too. Tomlin paying an old friend to hunt for Fern shows how desperate he is to give me the one thing I need in my life and, for that, I feel much closer to him than I did before I found out about it. I also feel guilty because I'm aware that I have not been an easy person to live with over these last few months, and that I should be more grateful Tomlin didn't just decide I was too much hard work and leave. He has not only stuck around but gone far beyond that, he's actively done something that makes me feel like the happiest woman in Arberness today.

He is very close to finding that bitch.

Now we know the fake name she is living under, it's surely only a matter of time until we find Fern. That's why I'm so glad that I was able to persuade Tomlin to keep this information quiet from the wider police force. That way, I can be the one who surprises Fern when we find her; rather me than some policeman who isn't as heavily invested in seeing that woman behind bars. An incompetent copper could inadvertently allow Fern to wriggle free again even if she is found, whereas I won't let her go.

Once I have her, she is mine.

With such a delicious thought to keep me occupied, it's little wonder I wasn't able to sleep much last night. But at least this time my lack of sleep is down to something other than my baby keeping me awake all night. I am perfectly okay with a few more restless nights if it ultimately ends with me grabbing hold of Fern and laughing in her face as I wrestle her to the ground and tell her that it's over.

Until such a time arrives, there is something else to keep me busy and, after putting Evelyn in her pram, where I suspect she will soon fall asleep once we start moving, I leave the house and head into the village. Tomlin is at work, but he'll be back home later tonight and, when he is, the first thing he will want to know is whether or not I attended the doctor's appointment I made yesterday. I will make sure to tell him yes, which will prove that I have kept my promise to him about speaking to somebody about how I've been feeling since Evelyn was born.

I can't say I'm looking forward to opening up and expressing my feelings to a medical professional but I know my boyfriend is right. I need to do it, for the sake of our relationship, my baby and for me. I don't know if I'm depressed or just struggling, but it can't hurt to get a few things off my chest and, who knows, maybe prescription pills might actually allow me to switch my mind off when my head hits the pillow at night.

I make it to the doctor's only having had to stop once when I bumped into the local butcher on the high street. He wanted to peep inside the pram and get a look at Evelyn. But now I'm here, right on time for my appointment, and as I enter the waiting room, I am ready to see the new doctor in the village.

His name is Doctor Andrews, and he is the man who was hired after the previous doctor was no longer able to fulfil his professional duties. Doctor Drew Devlin had a good reason for that, on account of the fact he had been murdered, but Drew's loss is Doctor Andrews' gain. While I know I will be in good hands with the new doctor, because I've already seen him before, back when I was pregnant with Evelyn and needed to discuss a few things. I also know the office he uses to conduct his work is one I have a very unique history with.

Whereas every other patient in this village goes into that room for a medical check-up and a chat with the doctor, I once went in there for something more.

I went in there to sleep with the doctor.

As my name is called and I enter the very familiar room, I glance at the bed where I once lay naked with Drew, my head on his bare chest as we talked after being intimate with each other. At the time, both of us thought that we had everything under control and that nobody knew about our secret liaisons.

Doctor Andrews catches me staring at the bed in the corner and clears his throat to get my attention and, when he has it, I apologise for daydreaming and take my seat beside his desk to get on with things. Then I start to feel paranoid that the doctor knows the reason I was just in such a trance. Does he? Is he aware that I slept with Drew in here? He might not be, but he will know that I was having an affair with his predecessor because everybody in this village knows that.

Oh God, this is so embarrassing. I need to get out of here. I can't do this.

Tears fill my eyes as flashbacks of Drew in this room come to me and it's clear I still have many demons to process when it comes to him. Before I can leave, Doctor Andrews puts a kind hand on my arm and tells me that everything is okay. Then he does the talking for me, pre-empting some of the things he thinks I might have been about to tell him by discussing how difficult parenthood can be and how past traumas especially can have a very negative impact on a new mother.

I usually hate the fact that my reputation around here precedes me but, in this instance, it seems it might actually be helping, because it's saving me having to go through everything with the doctor who is kindly looking to assist me today. It must be plainly obvious to him that I am struggling with my mental health. I do end up having to confirm that is the case as well as give a couple of examples of just how hard I am finding things with Evelyn. He then prescribes me some pills that should help with my moods, as well as referring me to a medical professional outside of this village who I can talk to more openly. That would be helpful, and I'm relieved about this because it's always going to be hard to be totally honest with a doctor who I could easily see down the village pub or on the high street at the weekend; talking to an outsider will be a big help. After thanking him, I take Evelyn and leave the room, heading for the chemist, which is only a couple of buildings away.

Once in there, I pass over my prescription to the smiling woman in the white coat and when she hands me my medication, I thank her and leave, pushing Evelyn outside while wondering if the small packet I hold in my hands is some kind of miracle cure for me. Doctor Andrews told me that it could take a while for me to notice any difference but the sooner I start on them, the better. So I do just that, popping a pill and swallowing it down before heading on my way.

As I turn the street corner to cut through the centre of the village, I presume I will see a few friendly faces as I make my way home. However, all that happens is that I see someone I was not expecting to see at all and, when I do, I let out an almighty squeal.

'Siobhan!' I cry when I spot my friend from prison standing

outside the butcher's talking to a local resident. When she sees me, she quickly excuses herself from the conversation before running over to me and the pram.

'Hey! Surprise!' she says before she opens up her arms and takes me in a hug. As we squeeze each other, it feels amazing to see her again. She looks much better than she did the last time we were together, though that wouldn't be hard considering we were both wearing prison uniforms and our hair and makeup was the least of our worries. But now she looks to be thriving, her skin radiant, her green eyes bright, and despite not noticing so much before thanks to her unflattering attire behind bars, she is clearly in good shape.

'What are you doing here? I know you said you were coming, but I didn't know when!' I say as we break off from our hug.

'I know. I was going to say I was on my way, but then I decided to try and surprise you,' Siobhan tells me, beaming widely. 'I figured this was a small village, so my plan was to ask one of the locals where you lived and then surprise you at your house. But you found me first!'

'I can't believe this!' I say, genuinely shocked but in a good way. 'You have no idea how nice it is to see you.'

'Who do we have here?' Siobhan says as she turns her attention away from me and onto the little girl in the pram. 'You must be Evelyn. Oh my, aren't you a little cutie!'

I watch Siobhan fussing over my baby for a moment while still shaking my head in disbelief that she came to Arberness so soon after asking if it was okay if she could come and visit. But now she is here, I am very much looking forward to catching up with her, so I suggest we head home where I can make us both a cup of tea.

'Tea? I haven't come all this way to just drink tea with you. Please tell me there is a pub in this village of yours.'

I laugh as Siobhan looks around for any sign of a place that serves alcohol before telling her there is indeed a pub in Arberness.

'Great, then let's go!' she suggests. 'We can take babies in the pub, right?'

'Of course,' I say as Siobhan volunteers to push the pram, and with that we're on our way to the social hub in this village, which is The King's Head. When we get there I find us a table in the corner while Siobhan goes to get the drinks. Despite telling her that I'll just have a glass of wine, she returns with a full bottle.

'Cheers, mate!' she says after pouring us both a good measure, and we clink glasses. As I take my first sip, I think about how this is not quite the weekday afternoon I was expecting to have. I also think about how Doctor Andrews told me that I should not drink alcohol on the pills he prescribed me, but considering that I've only just started them I doubt I have to worry too much about that yet. Besides, I'll just have this one drink. I'll be sensible. I should be anyway because Evelyn is with us.

At least that was the plan anyway.

Unfortunately, as Siobhan and I chat, I can already tell it's going to become harder for me to stop at just one or two glasses. I get confirmation of just how hard I'm finding it to stop when Siobhan suggests another visit to the bar and I don't say no as she gets out of her seat to get me another drink. But as I watch her order, I'm apprehensive because I'm already aware that things are going to be tricky when I get home later today. That's because Tomlin wasn't happy about the idea of me allowing Siobhan to come and visit, citing her criminal record as good reason not to have her in the house and around my baby. I assured him it would be fine, but the way we left it I think he assumed it was not happening at all. Siobhan is here now, so I can hardly tell her to find somewhere else to stay. However, as I will be happy to remind him if need be, there's nothing to worry about because she's harmless, at least to everybody who is not her former boss. Yes, she tried to kill him, but she's served her time for that.

She's not a danger to us.

She's my friend.

Or at least that's what I believe.

FOURTEEN

TOMLIN

The news that my old friend, Ian, had made a critical breakthrough in the search for Fern did wonders for my personal life. Delivering such good news to Alice helped bridge some of our differences and ease some of the tension that had been growing between us. I know it could also go a long way to improving my professional life too, which is why it is more than a little frustrating that Alice persuaded me to keep things under wraps so that we could find Fern before anybody else.

I understand why she wants to do things this way but she's also not the one who has been reporting for work every day in a place where everybody is gossiping behind your back and looking at you with either sympathy or disgust. All my colleagues in the police force know I am the one who lost Fern in the first place, so I would love nothing more than to march into my office and say that I have redeemed myself by finding her again. Unfortunately, I can't do that yet because I've given Alice my word that I will let Ian close in on Fern before we make our next move. It would also seem strange because having been removed from Fern's case and assigned to smaller, more menial investigations, it would arouse great suspicion if I revealed I'd secretly been working on something I shouldn't have been all this time. Besides, based on how my superiors treated me when Fern first escaped, I'm not sure I want to give them good news anyway, and let them take all the glory, when they haven't done anything.

As a detective, I'm used to self-sacrificing – this job is all about putting other things before yourself and this is just another example of that. I suppose it will be worth it in the long run because, once we have caught Fern, I'll get all the kudos and respect then, and redeem my reputation, so it's just delayed gratification. By delaying it, I will have also made Alice love me a little bit more so it will be worth it in the end. Until then, I'll have to continue to just be known as the stupid detective who bodged the biggest case of his career.

I'm not going to let that get me down for too long though because I'm driving home from my latest shift and I have a bag full of Chinese takeaway food sitting on the passenger seat beside me. The aroma coming from the bag full of delicious treats is making my taste buds tingle and I know it will do the same to Alice when I walk through the front door with it. She has no idea that I have picked up a scrumptious surprise for us to eat this evening, but I have a feeling she won't mind too much that neither one of us has to cook. With a bit of luck, we can get Evelyn settled in her crib for a while and that will allow us to sit down together and enjoy our meal and catch up on the other one's day.

There should be plenty to catch up on.

While I have a few tales to tell from work, I know Alice will also have a few things to talk about because she was due to attend her doctor's appointment this afternoon. I know she was reluctant to go and discuss her mental health, but I'm sure she stuck to her word and went ahead with that appointment. I'm also sure she is feeling better for doing so. It's always good to open up to somebody and I expect Alice will be feeling much calmer when I walk through the front door in a few minutes' time.

I'm just passing through the centre of Arberness and am almost home when my phone rings. I frown because I was not expecting a call from the person trying to contact me. It's Ken, the landlord of the village pub, and while we are on friendly terms, he doesn't usually call me out of the blue. He only has my number in the first place because I mentioned to him once that I didn't know too many people in the village, and he obviously took pity on me and asked for my number so we could get together some time. That hasn't happened yet and, even when the time came for us to meet up, I presumed it would be in his pub because there's not exactly anywhere else for two men to go around here, which would mean he would actually be profiting from our meet up with all the drinks I would end up buying at the bar. Unless he will be allowing me to drink for free, which could be fun, although not so much fun the morning after.

'Hey, Ken, are you okay?' I say as I connect the call using my hands-free system.

'Oh, hi detective,' Ken says and the fact he uses my professional job title tells me this might not be a friendly call at all. While I told him that I didn't have many friends in this village yet, that didn't mean everybody here wasn't already well aware of who I was and what I did for work. Maybe the real reason for my lack of friends here is that many of them blame me for letting Fern get away.

'What's up?'

'I'm just calling because I'm a little worried about something. I'm sure it's nothing, but I thought I better tell you just in case you needed to come here and check.'

'What are you talking about?' I say, concerned now that something else has happened in this village that shouldn't have.

'It's Alice. She's in the pub.'

'What?'

'And she's got Evelyn with her.'

'What's she doing there? I thought she'd be at home.'

'She's here with a friend.'

'Who?'

'A lady called Siobhan.'

I recognise the name immediately and grit my teeth. It's Alice's friend from prison. The one who tried to kill a man. I heard she might be coming but not this soon and, besides, I thought I was pretty clear when I told Alice that I didn't want her staying with us and being around Evelyn.

'She seems lovely,' Ken goes on. 'It's just that...'

'What?'

'Well, Alice and Siobhan have been drinking rather a lot. With little Evelyn here, I just thought I'd check to make sure they would be able to get home okay.'

It was bad enough hearing that Alice had met up with Siobhan but they're both drunk too!

Drinking alcohol with an attempted murderer with a small child in the pub... What has gotten into her? In what world does she think this is a good idea anyway, never mind when she's the guardian of a small child? I knew she wasn't herself with everything that's been going on, but this is not what I would have expected from Alice.

Talk about being irresponsible.

'I'm on my way,' I say as I head for the pub.

When I get there, I quickly leave my car and run inside. Once in the pub, it doesn't take me long to spot Alice because it's not hard to find her.

She's the one singing loudly in the corner.

Clearly she's had too much to drink. I rush towards her, taking in the wine glasses on the table but also Evelyn in her pram. I see Siobhan too and, even though we haven't officially met yet, I have a feeling I'm not going to make the best first impression on her.

'Alice. What are you doing?' I ask and my girlfriend looks stunned to see me. Although once she knows I'm here, she smiles and tells me to get a drink and join her.

'I'm taking Evelyn home,' I say as I take ownership of the pram. 'When was her last feed? How long have you been in here?'

Alice tells me that everything is fine and then attempts to introduce me to Siobhan, who flashes me a big smile and extends her hand, but I ignore them both because I'm far too mad at them for drinking this much while in charge of a baby. Alice looks and sounds very intoxicated, which only seems worse when I notice the small bag from the chemist sitting on the table beside her wine glass.

'What's this? Did the doctor prescribe you something?' I say but Alice just shrugs. I check the pills and, when I do, I know they wouldn't have been offered unless the doc thought there was a problem. It's good that she has them now but in order for their benefits to be seen, I'm certain they shouldn't be mixed with alcohol.

'Come on. Stay and have some fun,' Alice tells me, but I ignore her as Ken approaches the table.

'Why did you keep serving her when she's clearly had too much?' I ask him, but he just apologises and says he hasn't been the one on the bar serving all afternoon.

Noticing that I want to leave with the pram, Alice goes to stand up but stumbles and ends up knocking over her drink as she tries to regain her balance. Everybody in the pub is looking now, which is why I lower my voice and whisper at my partner.

'You're making a scene. It's time to go home,' I say, but Alice is not having any of it and just puts her arms out towards me.

'Give me *my* baby,' she tells me while Siobhan sips her wine and watches on.

I immediately sense trouble based on Alice's inflection when she said, '*my* baby'. The last thing I want is for her to remind me and everybody else in here that I am not Evelyn's father and, technically, don't have much of a right to be taking her home.

'Alice, come on. If you want to stay and drink with your friend that's fine, but Evelyn shouldn't be here if you're drunk,' I tell her, hoping that is fair.

But it seems not.

'Give her to me,' Alice says again before reaching for the pram. I move it away, not keen on the idea of her holding the little girl considering she could barely stand up herself a few moments ago. But Alice doesn't stop trying to get Evelyn back from me and reaches into the pram again, although this second time, she almost loses her balance, which only reinforces my point about how unsuitable it is for her to be in charge of a baby in her current state.

'Look at you! You can barely stand up! Evelyn could probably walk better than you can right now!' I say, not intending to embarrass Alice in public, simply stating what I feel is true. 'Just leave her alone before you end up dropping her!'

Unsurprisingly, Alice doesn't take my comments well, and it seems like we're on the verge of a very awkward argument in a very social setting, which is not going to do either of us any favours. That's until Ken steps in, expertly inserting himself into the argument with all the skill and experience of a pub landlord who has been breaking up disputes in this venue for decades.

He tells Alice that babies aren't really allowed in the pub at this time of the day, which helps me out a lot but also stops this whole thing being about me just wanting to take Evelyn away from her inebriated mother. He also suggests that Alice and Siobhan order something to eat because they must be hungry now, which is a polite way of saying they need something to soak up the alcohol without telling them to stop drinking altogether.

I decide not to mention the Chinese takeaway that is going cold in my car; the whole concept of a nice meal with my partner tonight has already been lost. Siobhan mentions that she is hungry and Alice seems like she is warming to the idea of food. Ken makes it sound even more appealing when he tells her that she can relax without having the baby to look after now that I'm here, before he turns to me and whispers that he will make sure they don't have too much more to drink tonight.

With Alice calmer, it seems like a good time to make my exit, so I tell her that I will see her at home then head for the door, with Evelyn in the pram.

As I step outside the pub, I'm aware tonight has turned into a bit of a shambles and, while things are okay for the time being, this is not over yet. Alice and I are likely to argue when she gets home later and even more so if Siobhan is with her looking for a place to stay for the night.

As I look down at Evelyn, I can't help but think about how so many crazy things had to happen for me to have ended up in this situation right here.

Just like Alice, so many of my problems can be traced back to Fern.

All I can hope is that Fern has plenty of problems of her own at the moment.

At least that would be some kind of justice.

But does she?

FIFTEEN

FERN

Life can be very hard when you have a seemingly impossible problem to solve. But life can seem surprisingly easy when you find a solution to such a problem. I have a big smile on my face because today I solved a problem. And I think life is going to get much easier going forward as a result.

I needed a way of getting access to the money in Drew's offshore account without taking it out in my new name, heaven forbid somebody should see that. Having had the idea that I could ask my neighbour, Victoria, to do me a favour, I hadn't known if she would agree until I tried her.

That's what I did this afternoon.

And she said yes.

Broaching the subject as delicately as it deserved to be broached, I was able to get across to Victoria there was money I was entitled to access but it was money I had to be secretive about. Playing on my neighbour's experience when it came to having people from the past to avoid and a real reason to remain lying low, I asked if Victoria could possibly withdraw the money into her account for me and, if so, I told her I would be willing to make it worth her while.

Amazingly, Victoria said yes without me even mentioning the figure I was willing to give her for her assistance, but I'd almost known she was going to be on board with my plan straight away based on how caring and attentive she has been ever since I have known her. Not requiring me to go into too much detail about where the money was actually coming from and why I needed her help, Victoria simply told me that whenever I was ready, she would provide the bank account details for me to send the money to.

There was a moment where I felt incredibly guilty for not only asking her but also how nice she was being about the whole thing, because if my deepest fears were realised and the police were monitoring this account, she was on the verge of becoming embroiled in something very nasty. Detectives would be tracking her down to find out exactly who she was and why she was helping me. While I might get the opportunity to run before they found Victoria I'd be leaving her with a lot of explaining to do. She could tell them that she had no idea I was a wanted criminal, and that is the truth, but would they believe her?

I don't like to think about condemning an innocent and extremely helpful friend to a potential police investigation that might not end well for her, which is why I'm not going to think about it any more. I have no other choice. I need this money and Victoria has offered to help me, taking a risk herself by not prying and asking any questions, presumably because the assumption is that this transaction may not be entirely proper, but she's happy to help me, and especially if she can make some money out of it herself in the process.

Two friends helping each other. That's all there is to it. Besides, it's too late for worrying about the pros and cons of it all now.

That's because the money is currently transferring.

I sat with Victoria earlier in front of my laptop and,

together, we did what was necessary to move the money from Drew's account to hers. According to the terms and conditions of the offshore account, it could take up to twenty-four hours for the money to show in the recipient's bank, which means I didn't quite get the instantaneous gratification I was looking for. It also means that I have now had to put an awful lot of trust in Victoria because, barring sitting by her side until the money lands in her account, I am going to have to take her word that she won't just disappear with the funds.

I don't believe she would do that because that would mean she was screwing over both me and Cecilia, a baby she clearly adores. Just in case, I decided to increase the amount of money I was willing to part with for her helping me. Instead of £500, I made it £800, which is far more than I'd wanted to give up, but it seemed incredibly cheap of me to only give her a fraction of the small fortune I was getting for myself. To her credit, Victoria refused the offer and said she was just happy to help, providing that if I moved away I stayed in touch and visited with Cecilia from time to time. But after not only promising I would do that, I made sure to make it clear that she would be well compensated for this, and as Victoria left my flat she was well aware that all she had to do was stick to her end of the bargain and she would be £800 richer within the next day.

It's been an hour since Victoria left my flat and what have I done in all that time?

I've stood by my front door and listened out to make sure my neighbour wasn't packing her things and leaving with all my ex-husband's money.

So much for trusting her, but there is a fine line between trusting someone and being stupid. At the end of the day, I have only known Victoria for a short while so she could be trouble. I doubt it but I have to be on my guard, which is why I'm making sure she won't leave me high and dry by sneaking away as soon as that money might finally be in her account.

One thing that helps me is that Drew's account will notify his email account when the money has officially transferred, which means I'll know the second Victoria has it. That's useful, though it also means that if I want to know exactly when it happens, I'm going to have to stay up all night and keep refreshing the page on my laptop screen. Staying up all night would have been a problem at one time in my life, but as Cecilia cries to let me know she is hungry for milk again, I have a feeling I'm not going to struggle to manage it now.

One sleepless night coming right up.

After satisfying my baby's ever-growing hunger, I think about what can happen once Victoria withdraws the money from her bank. The world will open up to me and I'll be free to leave this place and rent somewhere nicer. It's hard to believe it as I look around this horrid flat but soon I will be out of here. I'll be far enough away and I won't have to listen to the damn dripping tap that still hasn't been fixed yet. But I won't be going too far. I want to stay in this village because it's nice and I have a good friend here now. Victoria will have her £800 to spend and I'll be happy to hang around and see what she chooses to treat herself to.

Conscious that I need to fight fatigue as I sit here and intermittently refresh my screen to see if the money has moved yet, I break up that repetitive routine by having the occasional browse through some of Drew's old emails. I think I've read everything in here that relates to Alice until I come across an email about a medical gala in Manchester. I recognise the event in question because it is associated with a nice memory I have of Drew, or at least it was until I read the email he sent to Alice referring to it. That's when the memory I have is instantly tainted, and despite supposedly being sat at my laptop tonight to keep checking on the bank account, I find myself forgetting all about that for the time being and instead focusing on another lie I have just uncovered.

Considering what has happened since this medical gala, I perhaps shouldn't be shocked that Drew betrayed my trust on another occasion, but it still hurts, even though he's dead. As I reflect on the night in question, I feel the calming sense that despite everything I have done and the situation I find myself in now because of it, there are only four words that come to mind when I think about my spectacular revenge plot.

It was worth it.

SIXTEEN

FERN

I study my reflection in the bedroom mirror and feel like I'm looking as good as I can for the evening ahead. I had my hair and nails done earlier and I also picked up a new dress for this occasion tonight. I have transformed my look, curling my dark locks, and I've been slightly overzealous with the eye shadow. I've experimented and quite like the effect, feeling like the extra makeup really accentuates my eyes.

Overall, I am ready to present the best version of myself shortly.

I'm feeling, and looking, like a glamorous doctor's wife.

I'm sure the doctor himself will approve.

'Are you nearly ready?' I call out to Drew before picking up my glass of wine and taking a sip, noticing after I have that I have left a red semi-circle of lipstick on the rim. There's no need to reapply my makeup because that was the effect I was going for: lots of red. And some of it will rub off on whatever my lips touch tonight because, as always, I like to leave my mark.

Drew hasn't answered me, but that might just be because

there is music playing in the house and I don't think too much of it as I rummage through the contents of my clutch bag and make sure I have everything that I need in there. Other than a few makeup accessories, there isn't much I'm required to carry. Drew will have his wallet for the taxi but once we get to tonight's venue the drinks are free, which is convenient, and I very much plan to overindulge at the open bar.

As Drew presumably finishes up admiring his own reflection in the bathroom mirror, combing his hair and adjusting the bowtie on his tuxedo, I think about the reason for the pair of us beautifying ourselves on this Friday night. We are attending a medical gala, a large and glitzy charity event that brings together all the finest doctors in the Manchester area for an evening of eating, drinking, networking and raising some urgently required funds for various worthy causes in the city. It will be great to be in a room full of all sorts of interesting people, from the doctors themselves to their partners. It will also be nice to feel like we are giving back because, between us all, we should raise tens of thousands of pounds for charity as we bid on various items at auction.

I had a look at the website for the event earlier and saw some of the things we will get the opportunity to bid on later and I already have my eye on one of them. It's a two-night stay for two in a five-star hotel in the Scottish Highlands and I'd love nothing more than enjoying that getaway with Drew. I can see us already, wandering around lochs and taking selfies in front of spectacular mountains before returning to the plush hotel and sitting by a roaring fire wearing nothing but fluffy dressing gowns and sipping on the champagne that was just delivered by room service. I expect that in order to win the hotel stay, we will have to overpay, but that's the whole point of these auctions – people with money giving it up for a good cause. That will only make winning the prize even better; us bidding for the hotel stay might see the money we spend paying for new medical equipment at a hospital nearby, and that's worth every penny.

As I finish checking my handbag, I feel content that Drew and I already do plenty for charity, but we can always do more. I can't wait to get to the gala tonight and learn about some fantastic causes we are fundraising for, all while savouring the champagne and nibbling on a few canapes, of course. Having stopped working and become a full-fledged housewife, events like these are a chance for me to socialise outside of my close circle of friends. It's why I look forward to them so much, it gets me out of the house a little more than I usually would, plus these occasions really are good fun once the alcohol has kicked in and everyone lets loose.

Who doesn't love a chance to mingle with a bunch of well-dressed, well-paid and well-mannered individuals?

'Drew! The taxi will be here in a minute. Are you nearly ready?' I call out, but there is still no answer from the bathroom so I turn the music off, just in case he has been answering me and I haven't been able to hear him. The house is silent and now I'm getting a little concerned, so I go into the bathroom to check my husband is okay. When I do, I see him standing over the sink looking at his mobile phone.

'Hey, I was talking to you,' I say, confused as to why Drew seems to be in such a daydream. 'Are you ready? We need to go in a minute.'

Drew finally acknowledges me then, probably because he has no choice now that I'm standing right next to him, but when he does, it isn't good news.

'I'm sorry. I've messed up,' he tells me and, for a second, I am gripped with anxiety as to what he might be about to say.

'What is it?' I ask, standing nervously in my newly acquired and very expensive dress, staring back at my dashing partner in his black-and-white tux.

'I got it wrong. I thought partners were invited tonight, but they're not. I'm really sorry but you can't come with me to the gala.'

Half of me is relieved that Drew's confession is not actually anything too serious. But the other half is now very annoyed that I have got myself all dressed up and excited for nothing.

'What? You're kidding, right?'

'Sorry, no. I've just double-checked the invite and it's just medical professionals, so partners are excluded. I'm really sorry, I should have checked more carefully.'

This is irritating to hear but I can also see that Drew looks very sheepish about this, so I feel like I can't be too harsh on him because it was a genuine mistake. However, that doesn't solve my problem of what to do tonight. That is until Drew has a suggestion.

'Why don't you call one of your friends and see if they fancy going out for a drink?' he says. 'Claire, maybe? It seems a shame for you to have got all dressed up for nothing.'

'Claire's away this weekend. Besides, I don't want to go out for a drink with a friend. I wanted to go out for a drink with you.'

I know saying such a thing won't be helping Drew's guilt about accidentally inviting me to something, but I've gone and said it anyway. Although it's only because I want him to know that I really was looking forward to spending a lovely evening in his company.

'I'm really sorry,' he says again. 'I wish you could come too. I'll make it up to you, I promise. We'll have a night out together next Friday night, just the two of us. Dinner and drinks. Maybe we could stay at a hotel too. What do you say?'

That does sound nice, so I say yes, but it still doesn't change the fact I'm going to be stuck home alone tonight, all dressed up with nowhere to go.

'Why don't you get a takeaway? The menu for that new pizza place is in the kitchen drawer,' Drew suggests before he goes back to checking his reflection in the mirror. As he runs his hands through his dark hair, I get the sudden impression that he's not quite as disappointed about me not coming with him as he was initially making out. I don't know why I get that suspicion but, as I keep my eyes on him as he prepares to leave the house, I can definitely see that he looks much happier than he should be about this.

'So you're just going to go on your own?' I ask him as he grabs his coat and keys. 'Do you think you'll have fun?'

'Well, I have to go because I RSVP'd,' he tells me. 'There'll be a nametag there with my name on it, so they'll know if I fail to show up at the last minute. I don't want to be rude. And I know several doctors there, so it will be okay.'

Drew's breezy response is cut short when he remembers he probably shouldn't be so relaxed about leaving me alone while he goes off to get drunk with a load of medical colleagues, so he extends the answer he just gave me.

'I'm going to miss you,' he says. 'I'll be back as soon as I can, but you know how these things can be. It might get late. I wouldn't wait up. I'll text you when I'm in the taxi home. Okay? Love you!'

Drew gives me a kiss on the lips, the same lips I spent ages applying lipstick to earlier. As he pulls away, I see his lips now look a little redder than they did a moment ago. But he doesn't care about that as he heads for the door and, after giving me a wave, he is gone.

I go to the window and watch him getting into the back of the waiting taxi before it drives away. Now I feel stupid standing in this dress so I should go and change out of it. The sinking feeling in the pit of my stomach prevents me from doing anything as practical as that. Instead, I start to entertain the idea of doing something very impractical.

I grab my phone but, unlike Drew's suggestion, I am not calling for a takeaway to be delivered. I am actually calling for a taxi and when it gets here I want it to take me to the venue for tonight's gala. The reason for that is because of a deep-seated fear I have, and the need to make sure it is not coming true.

I've always been afraid that Drew might cheat on me.

What if that is what he is really doing tonight?

Once the taxi is ordered, I try telling myself that I am over-reacting and that my husband was being honest. I've never caught him lying before so I should just trust what he said about him getting mixed up with the gala invites. But then I think of the time I found out he was texting an old university friend, a female who was very attractive and someone who surely did not need to be messaging my husband as much as she was. Drew said there was nothing going on and I believed him in the end but, for a moment, I was terrified that my perfect marriage and my perfect life was going to collapse around me. I thought I'd put that paranoia to bed, but I guess not, because now I'm leaving the house and heading for the taxi that has just arrived to take me to the gala I'm supposedly not invited to.

As the driver heads for the venue, I wonder what I hope to see when I get there. Ideally, there will be lots of single people mingling with not a partner in sight. If that's the case then Drew was telling me the truth and I can return home happy that my man is still being faithful. I won't know until I get there and it's an agonising fifteen-minute journey until I do.

By the time the taxi parks outside the venue, I am a nervous wreck and I wonder if I am going to make a fool of myself and embarrass Drew as he chats to a bunch of doctors about all sorts of boring work stuff. But no sooner have I departed the taxi than my worst fears start to be realised, because I can see several attendees walking inside and many of them have partners on their arms.

So much for this not being an event for couples.

Drew was definitely lying to me.

But what else has he been lying to me about?

Aware that I won't find any more answers if I stay out here, I wonder if I can get inside or at least find out if Drew is in there himself, possibly with some other woman on his arm who shouldn't be there. That's why I approach the door and, when I do, I see a smartly dressed and smiling woman with a clipboard. When she sees me, she asks for my name.

Hoping that my name is on the guest list because Drew told me he had confirmed our attendance weeks ago, I tell the woman who I am and she checks her notes.

'Ah yes, Fern Devlin, I have you here. And you're with Doctor Drew Devlin, correct?'

'Erm, well no. Is he not inside already?'

The woman frowns and checks her list before shaking her head.

'No, he isn't here. Is he not with you?'

He definitely isn't. As the woman looks at me awkwardly, I feel much worse on the inside than my outward appearance would suggest. I might be standing here in a glamorous gown, but my husband is not here in his tuxedo beside me.

So where is he tonight?

And more importantly, who is he with?

SEVENTEEN

FERN

PRESENT DAY

The flat I am sitting in now is a world away from that decadent gala. The way I look tonight is also in stark contrast to how I looked that evening, but things have changed a lot since then. What has also just changed is how I look at that night in question and what came after it. After seeing this email from Drew to Alice, in which he told her he would make an excuse and get out of attending the gala so he could go and be with her, I now know the full extent of his lies that night.

To this day, I still thought what happened that night had turned out to be nothing more than a big romantic gesture on my husband's part. Despite me standing outside that gala without my date and feeling like an idiot, things quickly changed. By the end of the night, all had been saved. Now I feel as stupid as I did when I stood in front of that woman with the clipboard and asked her if my husband was inside, and that's because I've just found out I've been lied to again.

After finding out Drew was not at the gala, there was little else I could do other than leave. Before I went back home, I called my husband's mobile because I thought it would be inter-esting to see what he told me he was up to when he answered. Would he lie and say he was having a great time at the gala, or would he get flustered and wonder why I was checking up on him when I should just be being the loyal, obedient and naïve wife who is sat at home eating a takeaway by herself? As it turned out, I didn't get my answer because Drew did not pick up his phone, which only served to turn my shock and paranoia into anger and frustration. That was why I made the possibly ill-advised decision to leave him a voice message in which I told him that I knew he wasn't at the gala and wanted to know exactly what he was doing tonight because he clearly wasn't where he said he was going to be. I think I may have even ended that voicemail with a warning to him that if he was cheating on me then I was going to take everything from him in a divorce. In hindsight, it was not very sensible of me to expose my position and tip him off to the fact I knew he had lied, but I was upset and angry and, as I'd been prone to do with him in the past, I overreacted slightly.

After leaving that explosive voicemail message on his phone, I had little choice but to take a taxi back home and, once there, I sat impatiently by the window and waited for Drew to return, my head filled with all sorts of scary thoughts as I waited. It was after ten o'clock when I saw a taxi parking outside the house and, by the time Drew had made it down our driveway, I was at the front door, demanding to know what was going on.

He was instantly apologetic, his hands up in front of him and a desperate look on his face while he told me to calm down and that he could explain everything. Figuring that would be the part where my worst fears were realised and he told me he was leaving me for another woman, I ended up being very shocked by what I heard next.

'Okay, I didn't tell you the truth tonight. I was trying to keep it a surprise, but I guess you need to know now, so here it is. I actually went to reserve us a table at that new restaurant that just opened in Manchester. You know, the super-exclusive one owned by that chef you like from the TV.'

'What?'

'I've been queuing up at restaurant for the last couple of hours to reserve our table. I wanted to surprise you with the booking for your birthday because I know you've said you'd love to go, but now you know why I lied tonight. I'm sorry, but I was just trying to be romantic.'

Just trying to be romantic? Really?

'Why did you have to go to the restaurant?' I asked him then. 'Why couldn't you just reserve online?'

'The website crashed earlier this evening,' Drew had replied. 'The demand was so high, I guess. Then I was trying to reserve on my phone while I was in the bathroom earlier, but I couldn't get through. Then I saw a few people online said the best thing to do was to go down to the restaurant itself and reserve directly, so that's what I did. I made up the story about you not being invited to the gala, but the truth is I didn't go either. I went to get you the reservation because I knew you'd love to go and it's practically impossible to get a table.'

'You got us a table?' I had asked then, wanting to see evidence of this supposed story.

'Yes,' Drew says with a smile. 'I got us a table.'

Looking back, I should have seen through Drew's story for the nonsense it was. However, at the time, having been so afraid of him possibly cheating and expecting him to come home with some very bad news, I had ended up being so pleased with what I had heard that I believed him. Besides, it seemed like such a concise and cohesive story that it couldn't have possibly been made up, right? Stupid me. It ended up being such a good lie that I believed it all the way until tonight. But now, after reading this email, I know he really was with Alice that evening.

Damn it, I came so close to discovering his affair all the way back then. Maybe if I had just kept digging then I could have ended it all that night and everything that has happened since might not have. Then again, maybe if Drew had come home and told me about Alice then I might have lost all control and killed him right there and then. If that had happened, I definitely wouldn't have been able to get away with it like I have since.

Reflecting back on just how good a liar Drew really was, I think about how even after that night he still had work to do to keep feeding the lie and covering his tracks. Knowing what I know now, he obviously did not go out to book a table for a restaurant that night, but we did still end up going to eat there a few weeks later. That means he must have somehow managed to get a reservation not long after we had that initially tense conversation in our hallway. Maybe he pulled a few strings, knew someone there or someone else who was going and paid extra to take their place. He had the money and the charm to pull something like that off. He must have thought he was so clever. I bet he did when we actually went out to the restaurant and had a very romantic evening, enjoying the meal as well as all the drinks before it. I feel so stupid as I think back on how many times I thanked him for booking it and how he gratefully accepted all my compliments when I told him how romantic he was. *What a rotten pig.* All the time we were sat together across from each other at that table holding hands, I bet he was thinking about Alice and how he was getting away with seeing both of us.

Closing down that email because I don't want to think about him or her anymore, I notice there is a new message in his inbox and it's regarding the bank transaction I recently made. I see that the money has now left Drew's offshore account. That means it must be in Victoria's account now.

Should I go next door and check?

I'm seriously tempted to but then I look at the time and see that it is almost midnight, so there is a good chance I might wake her up if she has gone to bed. The considerate part of me tells me to just wait until the morning, although the paranoid part of me reminds me that Victoria could sneak off with all that money, and the paranoid part usually wins.

That's why, after ensuring Cecilia is safe and settled in her crib, I go to the door. I don't go out the front, opting to go out the back instead so, once outside, I can peer over the small wall between mine and Victoria's flat and see if there are any lights on. There are, and as I make sure to not be seen, I spot Victoria sitting on her sofa in the glow of the TV. It's a relief to see her still there rather than frantically packing, and I feel assured that she is not going to betray me. I also feel sad for her because she looks incredibly lonely in there, sitting all by herself. In that moment, I am as grateful as ever that I have Cecilia with me. Living on the run is tough but my baby is giving me the motivation to keep going. As long as I have her to fight for, I will never give up.

Returning to my flat, I lie down beside the crib and watch Cecilia sleeping. While I do that, I think about Drew and how he has never got to experience such a magical moment like this.

I bet if he had his time again he would have taken me to that gala.

Too late for that now.

Karma really does work its magic, I suppose.

But then I get an uneasy feeling because if such a thing as karma really does exist, does it mean something bad is going to happen to me soon?

I guess I'd deserve it.

Alice would certainly think so...

EIGHTEEN

ALICE

The room is spinning when I wake up and it takes me a second to figure out where I am. Once I have, I see that I am in my bedroom, which is strange because I don't remember getting here. Thinking about it, the last I recall I was at the pub with Siobhan and Evelyn. I'd been surprised that my friend from prison had arrived in Arberness so quickly after telling me she might visit. After she had met my baby, she suggested we go for a drink, which I agreed to.

So what happened after that?

I tentatively put a hand to my forehead but that doesn't ease the throbbing in my brain and, along with my headache, I have a little nausea to deal with too. I really do not feel in a good way and the longer I lie here and languish in this weary state, the more I try to answer one pressing question.

How much did I have to drink?

Every cell in my body is telling me that I probably don't want to know the true answer to that one, so I don't bother pondering it anymore. But as I go to get up off the mattress because I'm in desperate need of some water, I can't quite tell if I'm hungover or still drunk.

'Urgh,' is all I can say. I look at my bedside table and, when I spot my phone there, I pick it up to check the time. It's after midnight, which does nothing to calm me down, because as far as I can tell, there are several hours that seem to be lost to the deepest recesses of my mind.

However, at least I don't have to worry about Evelyn because there is a message here from Siobhan about an hour ago. She tells me that she helped put me into bed an hour ago and that she is sleeping on the sofa. She also tells me that Tomlin is looking after Evelyn and, while he wasn't too happy when we got back, he'll be okay in the morning.

I appreciate the message from Siobhan because, without it, I would be frantically running from this room to find out what happened to my baby. But after rereading it, I get a flashback of the argument I had at the pub.

Oh God. Tomlin turned up and he was angry. He had a go at me for drinking around Evelyn and he wasn't happy I was with Siobhan. Then he took Evelyn and left but not before we drew the attention of everybody else in the pub.

The regret and paranoia is strong, and I almost wish I hadn't been able to remember that. The brain often has a weird habit of making us remember the bad stuff and forget the good stuff and now I'm very much regretting what has happened. Why did I say yes to a drink at the pub? I should have known we wouldn't just have stopped at one. I really shouldn't have kept Evelyn out for so long. I also should have mentioned to Siobhan that my boyfriend wasn't too keen on her being around.

I know I've made mistakes and have some making up to do but, as far as I can tell nothing bad has happened. Evelyn is okay, which is the main thing, and according to Siobhan's message, she is sleeping here, so Tomlin must have relaxed a little bit and allowed her to stay the night.

What should I do now? Get up and find him and try to apologise? Or maybe I'm best leaving it until the morning?

Aware of how late it is, I decide to hold off on any grovelling yet because waking him and the baby up might be the final straw, so I roll over on the bed and hope that my headache eases off soon. Curled up in the foetal position, which is never a good position for a grown woman to find herself in, I think about the reason I overindulged so much at the pub. I could lie to myself and say I drank a lot because I was simply enjoying an old friend's company, but why bother? Better to just admit it to myself and say that having felt helpless and frustrated, both with Fern and Evelyn, I saw an opportunity to let loose and drown all my troubles in a sea of wine that Siobhan was mostly paying for.

I hope my friend is okay on the sofa tonight. She's probably passed out and will be okay tomorrow. I remember her telling me in prison that she rarely got hangovers, which was something for me to envy her for, just like I envied her when she was released from custody before I was. But it's been good to see her, and while I can't quite remember everything she has told me she has been up to since she got out, she seemed to be doing well for herself and it's nice that she came to see me. Hopefully I'll get the chance to have another chat with her in the morning and, this time, we'll be sipping nothing stronger than coffee as we talk.

Closing my eyes, I'm hoping I'll just drift off to sleep and when I wake up I'll feel like a new woman. But sleep is not a miracle cure, certainly not for my problems, and, as I discover, it's not even possible to drift off. I'm far too dehydrated and it's obvious to me that I need water and lots of it before sleep can even be an option for me.

Reluctantly forcing myself out of bed, I am at least spared having to look around my dark bedroom to find some clothes to put on because I'm still dressed in what I was wearing at the pub. I haven't woken up in yesterday's clothes since I was in my early twenties and a regular part of the Manchester city centre nightlife, but I guess I've reverted momentarily back to my younger days when this was a common occurrence. It's quite a sobering thought to realise that I seem to be going backwards in life, not forwards, but one thing at a time.

I want to get my life back on track and that all starts with a big glass of water from the kitchen tap.

Carefully opening my bedroom door, I creep out onto the dark hallway and listen out. But all is quiet so I carry on, passing the closed door to the spare bedroom where Tomlin and Evelyn are sleeping and onto the stairs. I'm amazed I can't hear the sound of a baby crying but am also super grateful for it because that's the last thing my headache needs. It also tells me that Tomlin is much better at getting my daughter settled than I am, but I knew that anyway.

Quietly descending the staircase, my dry throat is still desperate for water but, first, I know I'll have to make it past Siobhan on the sofa without waking her up either. Creeping around in the dark, especially while half-drunk, half-hungover is not easy, like some cruel kind of challenge that I do not need, but I am trying my best to be considerate of everyone else in the house. But it's as I get halfway down the stairs that I hear a noise, causing me to freeze.

I didn't cause the noise, nor is it one I would expect to hear. It's not a creaky floorboard, which wouldn't be an unusual thing to hear at all in this old cottage. Instead, it is something very peculiar. It's only when I bend down a little bit to get a good view of the living room that I understand what is going on in my own home.

Siobhan is on the sofa as she should be, but she is not alone.

Tomlin is with her.

And that sound I can hear is the two of them kissing.

NINETEEN

TOMLIN

When I got home tonight, I thought I was the one in the right and Alice was the person who had made some big mistakes. But as I get into bed and close my eyes to signal the end of this very long day, I know that I am not perfect myself and mistakes have been made on both sides. The only difference is that while Alice's mistakes were made openly in that pub earlier, mine remain secret.

Or at least I hope they will.

As I glance at the sleeping baby in the crib beside my bed in this spare room, I can't help but wish I'd just stayed in here with the resting Evelyn. If I'd done that then I wouldn't have a guilty conscience now. As it is, I left this bedroom and went downstairs earlier to get a drink. I descended those stairs as a loyal and loving boyfriend, but I climbed back up them as a cheating, lying love rat.

What the hell was I thinking, sleeping with Siobhan? I know she was still drunk from her exploits at the pub with Alice earlier today, but what excuse have I got? I'm stone-cold sober, which might make this worse because I can't blame my indiscretion on alcohol.

As I lie on my back and stare up at the ceiling, listening to the quiet house around me and thanking my lucky stars that both Alice and Evelyn have slept through the last few hours, I reflect on the craziness of what just happened.

After taking Evelyn from Alice in the pub, I came back to the house and got the baby fed, bathed and ready for bed. During that time, I kept an eye on the clock, wondering when Alice would come home. It was late when she did and, as I already knew she would be, she was extremely drunk, as was the woman she was with. But at least Evelyn was having a peaceful night and, after getting her settled, I decided not to cause too much drama when the ladies got home. I simply suggested that Alice go to bed and Siobhan sleep on the sofa and we could talk in the morning.

Both women seemed happy enough with that so we all went to our beds, and I thought that was where the night would end. That was until just after midnight when I suffered a bit of a coughing fit and needed water, only to realise I didn't have any in the room.

I'd gone downstairs, planning on being quiet and not disturbing Siobhan, in case it led to an awkward conversation between me, the detective, and her, the ex-convict. But having got to the bottom of the stairs, I found Siobhan sitting up wide awake and, when she saw me, she immediately apologised for what she had done.

It turned out she had found more alcohol in the fridge and carried on drinking by herself.

In that moment, I was seriously tempted to tell Siobhan that she had to leave because, as far as I was concerned, she was a terrible influence on Alice. She had committed a serious crime and she was also a serious drinker, so what good could such a person be for my girlfriend or her baby? Then I imagined me and Siobhan arguing loudly and Alice and Evelyn waking up and that sounded like an even bigger problem, so I simply told

Siobhan it was fine and went into the kitchen to get my water. I
had not been expecting her to follow me in and after she apologised again, this time for keeping Alice out so late, I had no
choice but to accept that too. Maybe it was because I'd been so
understanding that Siobhan decided she'd like to share a drink
with me. She offered, although I did say no, planning to just go
back to bed and get some sleep.

That was until Siobhan said she was worried about Alice
and wanted to talk.

Foolishly taking a seat on the sofa with Siobhan, I let my
guard down and had a drink while Siobhan told me how tough
Alice had found it in prison. Maybe I'd been hoping to hear
something that might help me find a way of getting through to
Alice a little better, or maybe I was just enjoying the company
of a woman who was not always arguing with me. Whatever it
was, I relaxed more and more and, after a while, I was feeling a
little guilty that I'd been so harsh towards Siobhan. As a detective, I'm taught to see everything as right or wrong because, with
the law, there are no grey areas. But that has often led to me
being very narrow-minded. As Siobhan showed a funny and
caring side to her character, I realised there was far more to her
than her criminal record.

She was a good friend to Alice.

Or at least that was what I thought.

As one drink turned into two, Siobhan moved the conversation away from the woman sleeping upstairs and we discussed
our own lives. Being slightly flirty and more than a little suggestive, Siobhan had hinted that the hardest thing about being in
prison had been missing the company of men and she told me
she was jealous of Alice for having someone like me to look after
her. I know I should have been more guarded but I was simply
enjoying the compliments and the flirting too much to put a
stop to it. Before I knew it, I was getting dangerously close to
Siobhan. Maybe if relations with Alice had been better over

these last few months I might not have felt so drawn to another woman, but one thing led to another, and we ended up kissing before going even further than that.

I can't speak for Siobhan, but I do know that I felt guilty as soon as it was over. I gathered up my clothes and scurried away upstairs, although just putting some distance between me and the scene of my affair isn't making me feel much better. That was so out of character for me, and I feel rotten. I feel even worse when I think about everything Alice has been through, because her finding out that I had cheated on her with her friend from prison might be the final nail in the coffin as far as her and her fragile mental health goes.

That is why she can never find out what happened.

I didn't need to tell Siobhan how important it was for this to remain a secret, and hopefully it will always stay that way. I do care about Alice, despite what just happened, so I'm hoping I can put this down to a moment of weakness and move on, for my sake, Alice's and, of course, little Evelyn. There's nothing quite like the innocence of a child to put into sharp contrast the shame of a disgraced adult and, as I lie on the bed and look at Evelyn, I wish I had never gone downstairs.

I hope to fall asleep then but as is the case with a guilty conscience, sleep is impossible, so I pick up my phone and send a message to Ian, asking for an update. I haven't heard from him for a while, not since he told me he had the name Fern was now living under. I don't expect him to message me back straight away because it's the middle of the night, but I press send anyway and then wait for his reply all the way to sunrise.

It's just after six when I see the light coming through the curtains and it's not long after that when I see a new message flash up on my phone.

It's from Ian and he does have an update.

He says he made a major breakthrough late last night and wanted to call but thought it was late, so he was waiting until the morning. Now that time has come, he can give me the news without fear of waking me up.

He tells me that after looking into several Teresa Browns living in the UK, he has been able to narrow his search down to one place that he thinks has potential.

While it's not been confirmed yet, according to him and his vast experience in finding people who didn't want to be found, he thinks he knows the area where Fern is.

He thinks she is in Cornwall.

We're close now.

So close, yet still so far...

TWENTY

FERN

Despite planning to stay up all night to make sure Victoria didn't do a runner with my money, I must have ended up falling asleep for a couple of hours because, when I wake up, the sun has risen and Cecilia is crying in her crib, clearly ready for her first feed of the new day. Before I feed her, I scramble to the door and rush outside, terrified that Victoria has gone, as well as my money and my last hope of escaping this grim place.

Knocking on her door, I am praying that she answers while simultaneously imagining myself having to take Cecilia and go running through the centre of the village calling out for my neighbour and hoping to catch her before she boards a bus or train out of here. But there is no need for any of that because Victoria's door opens and when it does, I see her smiling at me.

'Good morning,' she says, a half-eaten piece of toast in her hand. 'Is everything okay?'

'Er, yeah, fine! Good morning. I was just going to check if the money had gone in.'

'It has,' Victoria replies before taking another bite of her breakfast. 'It's ready when you are.'

'Great!' I say. 'I'll just get ready and then we'll take a trip to your bank if that's okay?'

'No problem. Do you need help with Cecilia?'

I'm just about to say that I'll be okay but then figure it can't do any harm if Victoria comes back to my place where I can keep an eye on her, so I thank her and say yes if she wouldn't mind. She quickly stuffs the rest of her toast into her mouth before grabbing her handbag and following me back to my flat.

While I feed Cecilia, Victoria very kindly tidies up a few things, making my surroundings a little more bearable, and once my baby is ready to go, I quickly get changed and I'm ready too.

The plan now is to go to the bank where Victoria will attempt to withdraw as much money as she can from the new funds that went into her account overnight. By visiting the branch in person, there is a better chance they will give her more money than simply withdrawing the funds from a cash machine, because they usually have more stringent limits. So, fingers crossed, a decent chunk of the money can come out and I can pay Victoria the fee I have agreed to give her for her troubles.

But I'm worried the bank might ask her why she needs to withdraw so much money, so we have made a plan for that. Victoria is going to say that she has inherited the funds and is planning to use her windfall to put down a deposit for a second-hand car and the dealer has asked for cash if possible. It's not unusual for vehicles to be purchased in such a way so I'm hoping the clerk at the bank won't make too much of a fuss, but we will see. All I can do is hope there won't be any last-minute hiccups with my plan.

'I'll push the pram,' Victoria says as we leave my flat and I'm happy to have a little break from that particular duty as we head for the bank, both our minds filled with visions of fifty-pound notes that are soon to be filling our purses.

It's a sunny day and the walk is a pleasant one as Victoria

and I talk about how, despite various difficulties in our past, we are lucky to live in a place where people pay good money to visit as tourists each year. But the seaside village vibe does also remind me of Arberness. Especially when I see the sign for the local butcher's or the way a couple of locals recognise each other on the street and stop for a chat, their shopping bags over their arm as they quickly gossip before getting on with the rest of their daily errands. It's funny because on the surface everything looks perfectly normal here but, once again, I'm aware that a crime is about to take place and, as usual, I'm right at the centre of it.

By the time we reach the bank, there are a few butterflies fluttering in my stomach because I'm still not sure how this is all going to play out. That's why I decide to give Victoria a little pep talk before she goes inside and leaves me waiting out here with Cecilia.

'Remember, they might not simply hand over the money. They might have a few questions, so just stay calm and stick to what we discussed, okay? And if at any point you think something might be going wrong and they are taking more time than they should, just thank them and leave. We can always try and figure it out later, but we don't want the police to come here and start asking questions because that could make things tricky for the both of us.'

I'm hoping adding that last part about 'both of us' will emphasise that we're in this together now. I didn't need to worry about that because Victoria is more than ready to go.

'I'll be back out soon,' she says breezily before striding confidently into the bank. I guess there's nothing more I can do than hope for the best, so I distract myself by pulling silly faces at Cecilia for the next few minutes while other customers come and go.

It's an anxious wait and, while I'm keeping one eye on the door, I'm also keeping a lookout for any sign of police cars arriving here. But so far so good and when I do see the door to the bank open again, Victoria emerges, and she has a big smile on her face.

She has something else too.

My money.

'Sorry, there was a big queue in there, but I got it,' Victoria says with a smile, holding up the bulky envelope filled with fifty-notes.

'They gave you all of it?'

'No, only £10,000. I'll have to go back for the other half tomorrow but that's okay, isn't it?'

'It's fine,' I say, just relieved that it worked. And relieved that I have fifty per cent of Drew's money now.

'There you go,' Victoria says, handing the envelope over with a smile before looking down at Cecilia and cooing at her.

While she's focusing on my baby, I'm focusing on the cash in my hand. I suggest we leave the busy high street and go home so we can sort the funds out and I can give Victoria what I owe her. But she has another idea.

'Seriously, don't worry about the money, I'm just happy to help,' she tells me. 'I'd rather you spend it on yourself. When was the last time you had a break and treated yourself to something? Why don't you go and get your hair or nails done?'

Thinking about it, I have not had any break at all since my baby was born and, now I have the money, a much-needed makeover would be lovely.

'What about Cecilia?'

'I can look after her. I could walk around the park with her.'

It is a nice day and Victoria is good with Cecilia so I think that plan might work. The more I think about it, the more it would be nice to treat myself. There is a nail salon nearby that I have so far only walked past but it would be good to go in and spruce up my very shabby looking nails. But can I?

'I don't know. Maybe we could all go for lunch together.

The three of us. My treat,' I suggest, feeling like I have to do something for Victoria when she has just done something for me. But all she seems to want is for me to relax.

'It's fine, honestly. Just go and do whatever you want to do for the next hour or so and come meet us in the park after. We'll be fine, won't we?'

Victoria is talking to Cecilia then who giggles as my neighbour strokes her cheek. Seeing as my baby looks so happy, I feel better about leaving her for a short while. Besides, who knows when I might get the chance again?

'Okay, if you're sure?' I ask, checking one last time.

Victoria nods and, with that, I give Cecilia a kiss goodbye before telling my neighbour that I'll be at the nail salon and she is to come and get me if she needs me at any time. Victoria agrees before pushing the pram away in the direction of the local play park. I have something I've not had for a long time.

Freedom.

Heading to the nail salon, I am thinking about what I might ask for when I get there. But by the time I have been warmly greeted by a beautician and sat down in a chair opposite her, I get a strange sensation that this wasn't a great idea. As much as I trust Victoria and as much as she has helped, I feel like I should stay with Cecilia rather than leave her with someone else, so I walk away and go in the direction of the park, expecting to catch them up before they even get there. I don't see them, so I walk through the park gates and look around for a woman pushing a pram. There are a few people with children in prams but none of them are Victoria, so I keep walking along the path that loops around this park. But by the time I get back to where I started, I haven't seen my neighbour or my baby and then I start to get worried.

Victoria said they would be here, so where are they?

Figuring they might have gone into a shop, I head back for the high street but, as I do, I take out my phone to give Victoria a call. But she doesn't answer and after running along the high street and still not finding any sign of her, I suddenly start to panic.

What was I thinking? Why did I leave Cecilia with her?

Maybe she couldn't be trusted.

And now it's too late to have realised that.

TWENTY-ONE

ALICE

It was a long and lonely night as I lay on my bed and thought about what I'd seen going on downstairs between my boyfriend and my friend when they thought I was asleep.

Tomlin has cheated on me and instead of being the mistress in an affair I am now the victim.

So this is what it feels like.

Despite having the awful image of Tomlin and Siobhan kissing on the sofa still burnt into my mind, there was another image that came to mind. It was one of Fern. Now I know what it's like to suffer the shock of finding out my partner is cheating; I know what she must have felt like when she discovered her husband was sleeping with me.

That means I have some sympathy for her, which is not something I ever thought would be possible. However, a little sympathy is as far as it goes because, despite what I now know, I am not thinking about murder or framing innocent people for crimes they didn't commit. I'm not a monster, unlike Fern who went way beyond what she had a right to do to get her own back. I'll still never forgive her for what she did to me. But while I might not be willing to go to such extremes to get revenge on a cheating couple, there is no doubt that I want to do something to Tomlin and Siobhan for betraying my trust.

As of yet, neither of those two know what I saw, which means I expect they will both behave as if nothing happened when I go downstairs to see them shortly. While they can pretend all they want, I know the truth, and the only question now is what am I going to do about it?

Taking off the clothes from yesterday that I slept in, I quickly shower before seeking out the other people in this house, though I am only looking forward to seeing one of them. When I do find Evelyn, I give her a big kiss and a cuddle, which is not something I can say I've always done first thing in the morning, usually because she has given me a torrid night of no sleep. But I'd much rather be warm to her than to the two people standing in my kitchen. Tomlin and Siobhan each have a cup of tea and, when they see me, they do exactly what I thought they would, which is act like they didn't do something wrong in the middle of the night.

'Good morning, sleepy head. How are you feeling?' Siobhan asks me, putting a big smile on her face. 'We drank so much yesterday!'

'I'm fine,' I mumble before looking to Tomlin who seems just as awkward.

'The kettle has just boiled. Would you like a coffee?' he asks me.

I nod my head, allowing him to busy himself with that simple chore rather than look at me and feel bad about what he has done.

As he makes my coffee, Siobhan compliments me on my home before going to Evelyn and fussing over her for a moment. I can't believe the cheek of this pair for pretending like they are on my side. If me and my baby weren't here now then these two would probably be back to doing what they were up to on the sofa last night, rather than acting like my best friends.

'We need to talk,' I say to Tomlin just after he hands me my coffee and that's an understatement, but he's probably thinking my request is about nothing more than what happened at the pub yesterday when he stormed in and took Evelyn from me. Considering what has happened since then, Tomlin seems to have conveniently forgotten about that and tells me that he is sorry for overreacting before suggesting something.

'It's market day today. How about we go and have a walk around?'

'That sounds good!' Siobhan says quickly in agreement. While I watch her playing with Evelyn, I wonder how long she is hoping to stay here for. Before last night, I would have been happy to accommodate her for several days because I thought it was nice to have her around. Now I think she is only lingering because she is hoping to get another private moment with my man, or at least the person who thinks he is my man until I decide what to do with him.

'Okay,' I say, willing to go to the markets because it has to be better than being cooped up here with lots on my mind. But before we leave, I go back to my bedroom and, once in there, I pop a couple of the pills that the doctor gave me yesterday. I'm only supposed to take one a day but screw it, if these are going to help lift my mood then I need as many of them as I can get.

I hope the medication kicks in soon but for now I have nothing but a hangover and the shock of what I saw to languish in for the time being. The four of us leave the house and head for the centre of the village. Siobhan volunteers to push the pram and I allow it because I'm simply too tired to do it myself, but my eyes are burning into the back of her head as we walk. I feel just as much hatred for the person next to me, but I am surprised when he leans in and whispers something to me on the way.

'I have something to tell you,' he says, which is surprising because I wonder if he is going to confess his infidelity to me.

That's something Drew never had the bravery to do with Fern, not that it's a particularly heroic thing either way.

'What is it?' I ask him as I keep watching Siobhan ahead of us.

'I'll tell you when Siobhan has gone,' he says. 'When is she leaving, by the way?'

That's a good question.

'I'm not sure,' I reply, because that's the truth. 'Why can't you tell me now?'

'It'll be very distracting for you, and I don't want to spoil your fun with your friend.'

Spoil my fun with my friend? I think it's a little too late for that.

'Distracting?'

'I'll tell you in a little while. Let's just enjoy the morning,' Tomlin says before we turn the corner, and the high street comes into view. When it does, I see rows of market stalls, all selling various wares, and Siobhan comments on how pretty it looks. She then says something very troubling.

'I love it here! Maybe I'll move!'

My stomach churns at that sentence and it makes me want to end this charade right now. But we're in a public place, plus I have to be careful for two reasons. One, if I expose their affair, that might be it for me and Tomlin. I'm not sure I want that yet because, as much as I hate him for cheating, I think I might hate being a single mother even more. I also could do with keeping him around at least until I have found Fern and he seems to have the resources to help me with that. And two, Siobhan is, as my boyfriend kept reminding me before she got here, a convicted criminal who is guilty of attempted murder of a former boss. That means she might not be the best person to be making an enemy out of.

'Wow, it's busy,' Tomlin says as he looks around, and he's not wrong. As usual, most people in the village have come out to support market day and many locals are perusing all the stalls while a few pause to make a purchase. There are a few faces I don't recognise, so they might be tourists stopping off for a look around and they've picked a good day for it because the weather is nice and there's plenty to see and do here.

As one of the ladies who works at the local supermarket comes over to see Evelyn in her pram, Siobhan is still the nearest to my baby and she beams as she gets to show her off. But she's not hers, she's mine, and when Tomlin moves beside her and shares a smile with them both, I suddenly feel over-whelmed at the situation.

Perhaps it's because I'm in a very crowded place. Perhaps it's because I'm severely hungover. Maybe it's because I saw what I saw in the middle of the night and now feel like even more of a victim than before all the craziness with Fern started. Or maybe it's because the chemicals in my brain have just been altered by the pills I took this morning. Whatever it is, my legs feel very weak and I find myself falling to the floor. I've not quite fainted but I know it won't be easy to get back up again.

A few people gasp when they see me fall before rushing to my aid, but it's Tomlin and Siobhan who are first to help try and get me back to my feet.

'What happened? Are you okay?' Siobhan asks me before Tomlin suggests that I'm moved towards the nearest bench. Once they have set me down in a more comfortable position, I have the chance to process what just occurred.

Looking around, it feels like everyone at the market is staring at me and I bet I know what most of them are thinking.

Poor Alice. She has never been the same since Fern came here. That woman ruined her life. I'd be a mess too if I was her, especially because Fern has gotten away with it all.

That's why I start crying and, as the tears flow, it at least makes a few people feel bad for gawking at me and some of them turn away to pretend like they are going to carry on with what they were doing before I made a big scene. Tomlin is still by my side, and as he grips my hand, he asks me what is wrong.

I'm too upset to speak and I'm assuming he's about to suggest that we go home, and I have some rest. But that's not what happens. Instead, he tells me how brave I have been before saying that he should have told me the news sooner.

'What news?' I ask him and then he gives it to me.

'I know where Fern is,' he says. 'I'm still waiting for a definite address, but we have a location. She's in Cornwall.'

Just like that, my tears stop, and I feel like a new woman as I stare at the man beside me.

'You've found her?' I say and Tomlin nods his head.

'Yes, we have,' he replies with a big smile. 'We're not quite there yet, but we're closing in on her, and I promise you she won't get away this time. Does that make you feel better?'

I don't have to think for very long about my answer to that one. That's because I'm smiling now too.

'Yes, it does,' I say as my tears quickly dry, and my mind is already on one thing and one thing only.

I want to get in the car, and I want to start driving south.

I want to get to Cornwall as quickly as possible.

When I get there, I want to see Fern's face when I tell her this is over and I have won.

TWENTY-TWO

FERN

I'm running around the village, crying out for my baby and hoping that somebody can help me, but so far, nobody can. Half the people I pass want to assist but then quickly realise they can't – they haven't got a clue who might have my baby and where they might be now – while the other half simply stop and stare, appearing dumbfounded as I rush past them with a frantic look on my face. The only thing that will make me feel better is if I see Cecilia and know she is okay, but I can't find her anywhere, despite racing all over and looking for her in every direction.

I now think that Victoria exploited the trust I put in her and has abducted my child. If that is the case then I may never see my baby girl again. If that is true then I'm not sure I want to live, but I have to fight and use what little strength is left in my body to try and save my tiny daughter, and myself.

The obvious thing for any parent to do in this situation would be to call the police. But I'm no normal parent; while the police usually help people, they are the enemy to me. I can't risk having my true identity exposed so I won't call them, because even if they were somehow able to find Cecilia for me, what good would it be if they figured out who I was? They would take me away and I'd only end up losing my baby all over again.

There is someone I can try and call. I try Victoria's phone one more time, but there's still no answer and then I give up on that because it's obvious she has no intention of answering.

Why would she if she is trying to get away?

Wait, that's it.

If Victoria has abducted Cecilia then she must have gone back to her place to grab a few of her things.

Suddenly having a destination to target rather than aimlessly running around, I sprint in the direction of home, and it doesn't take me long to get there at the pace I'm sprinting. As the flats come into view, I have no time for worrying about the dodgy youngsters hanging around on their bicycles nor do I worry about the smelly rubbish piled up in various places on my way. I just rush to Victoria's door and then begin banging on it, pounding my fists into the plywood and feeling fully prepared to break through it myself if I have to.

Maybe I'm already too late and Victoria has grabbed her things and left. Or maybe she decided not to risk coming back here at all and is on the move with Cecilia because that's the quickest way for her to disappear without me catching up with them. I have no answers and I'm terrified that I will never get any, but then it's as if all my prayers are suddenly answered because the door opens and I see Victoria standing in front of me looking like there is nothing wrong at all.

'Hey! What's going on? I thought you were getting your nails done?' she asks me, looking puzzled but nowhere near as stressed as I am.

'I thought you were going to the park! I was trying to find you!' I cry, before looking past my neighbour in search of Cecilia. When I see my child in her pram, looking sweet and unharmed in her pink dungarees and smiling because she recognises the sound of her mother's voice, it's as if the vice-like grip across my chest is released.

'Sorry, I thought it was a bit too windy, so I decided to come back here with her. I was going to bring her back to meet you just before you were finished.'

I look at Victoria and guess she is telling me the truth because she is here and not running away right now with my baby in her arms.

'I'm sorry,' I say, suddenly feeling embarrassed. 'It's just it's the first time I have left her with anyone and I guess I freaked out a little bit.'

'That's perfectly understandable,' Victoria says with a warm smile. 'But as you can see, Cecilia is perfectly fine. Why don't you take a look for yourself.'

Victoria steps aside then, allowing me in. I walk right past her to my baby. Sure enough, she is right because Cecilia looks absolutely fine. Now I simply feel foolish.

'Maybe I'm just not ready to leave her yet,' I say as I shake my head as Victoria closes the door. 'I know I need to take a break but it's hard. She's all I've got.'

'I understand,' Victoria says, joining me by the pram. 'But she is safe with me. If you want to just go for a ten-minute walk and clear your head, that's okay. You can start small. Sorry for rushing you into thinking you needed to leave her for an hour or more.'

It feels good to be relaxed again and, even though I know this was a hiccup, I'm sure I'll be much calmer next time I decide to leave Cecilia's side for more than two minutes. But just as I'm starting to feel like everything is okay again, I notice something on Victoria's sofa.

It's an open suitcase and beside it is a pile of clothes.

'Are you going somewhere?' I ask Victoria as I think about how I didn't see that suitcase last night when I was sneaking around at the back and peeping through my neighbour's window.

'Oh that? No, I'm just tidying up. Throwing away a few old things, trying to make some more space in here.'

That sounds legit, but why does Victoria suddenly look so shifty?

'Seriously, if you want to just go for a walk around the block or something to clear your head. I'm fine here with Cecilia for ten minutes,' she tells me but I'm getting the sense that something else is going on here. After looking again at the suitcase, I take a couple of steps back in this tiny flat in order to take a peek into Victoria's bedroom and, when I do, I see the wardrobe doors are wide open, as are all the drawers. That might not be particularly concerning if it wasn't for the fact that all these items of furniture are empty now, totally devoid of any clothing, which makes me confused about what my neighbour just told me.

She said she was having a tidy up.

So why is she packing everything?

'What's going on?' I ask Victoria as I turn back to her but, when I do, I see that she has picked Cecilia up out of her pram and is cradling my child.

'Why did you have to come back here?' she asks me. 'Why couldn't you have just gone and got your nails done like you said you were going to, and everything would have been okay.'

'What?'

'I don't want any drama and I'm sure you don't either. Not in your situation.'

'My situation. What are you talking about?'

'Drop the act,' Victoria says with a sigh. 'I know who you are.'

Those words are chilling to a person on the run, so I decide not to say anything in case there is a chance that Victoria is talking about something else.

'Who I am? I'm Teresa,' I try.

'No, you're not,' Victoria replies with a smug smile. 'You're Fern Devlin. You're the doctor's widow. Or should I say, the Black Widow.'

I'm frozen as I try to figure out how Victoria could possibly know my real identity. More than that, I'm trying to figure out why my friendly, caring neighbour now seems so cold towards me.

After quickly trying to think of the best thing to do, I opt to burst out laughing in the hope that it will make Victoria think that this is all one big misunderstanding.

'Oh, you're playing a joke on me. Good one. Very funny,' I say with a smile. 'You almost had me there.'

But Victoria isn't laughing. All she is doing is continuing to hold on to my baby.

'I'm serious, Fern. I know who you are and what you did. The police are looking for you, aren't they? That's why you're living here in this place under a fake name. You're trying to hide from them. It's why you needed my help with the money, isn't it? You couldn't risk just taking it out yourself in case something went wrong, so you used me. It's okay, I'm not mad. I understand. But I do know exactly who you are, so stop playing games with me.'

That seems to be my cue to drop my failing act, so I do just that, holding up my hands in front of myself to try and pacify the person who I thought was my friend.

'Okay, yes, you're right. I am Fern, but I can explain! I wasn't using you. You're my friend. You offered to help me. And don't believe everything you have heard in the news. Those journalists have exaggerated everything. I'm not dangerous. I'm just trying to give the best life I can to my baby.'

Victoria rolls her eyes at that, but I have to make her believe me. I also have to know how she figured this all out.

'How did you know?' I ask her nervously. 'When did you find out?'

'I found out when I did an internet search for the name on the bank account that you were transferring money from,' Victoria says. 'I thought the name D Devlin sounded familiar, so I typed it into Google and when I did, all sorts of crazy results came back. Articles about a murder and a trial and a wife on the run. Then I knew where I had heard that surname before. I'd heard it in the news. I also knew what the 'D' stood for then. It's Drew, right. Drew Devlin, the dead doctor in Arberness. It's his bank account and his money and the only reason you knew about it is because you are his wife. You're the one who the police think killed him.'

Victoria is right about absolutely everything, but what am I supposed to do? Congratulate her on her investigative skills and tell her it's no big deal that she's actually been living next door to a wanted criminal all this time?

'You're on the run and you needed that money to stay on the run,' Victoria goes on. 'It's okay, you don't have to hide it from me. I know the truth now, so just relax. I'm not the police, so you're not in trouble. Not yet anyway. But you could be because all I have to do is make one call and they will be here in five minutes to arrest you.'

'Don't call the police,' I beg, stepping towards Victoria but she steps back, as if I pose a threat to her and to the baby she is holding. Of course I'm not a threat to Cecilia, but as for Victoria? Well, this wouldn't be the first time I have been pushed into a corner and had to fight my way out of it. Maybe I should remind my neighbour of that. But that's a last resort and I'd prefer to resolve this peacefully for the sake of my daughter, so I calm down like Victoria suggested before trying again.

'You've helped me. You've been a great friend. I appreciate that and I appreciate that you haven't called the police already,' I say, maintaining a respectful distance between us so as not to look intimidating. 'Thank you. I don't have any other friends, so I need all the help I can get.'

'I'm not surprised. A woman like you must find it hard to make friends when you leave a trail of dead bodies in your wake.'

'It's not as simple as that! I was pressured into things. I was upset. Angry. Confused. I regret everything I've done, but I can't change it. All I can do now is try to be the best mother I can be to my baby. You understand that, right? Cecilia needs me. It's not fair on her if I go to prison. She'd be alone. Please, I'm just trying to live a good life. A normal life. I'm just trying to start again, just like you.'

'I'm nothing like you,' Victoria says coldly and that's the moment when I realise she really isn't my friend anymore. Despite her not calling the police, there is clearly a different ending that she wants. She isn't going to agree to me just taking Cecilia and going back to live next door as if nothing happened.

'Okay, what do you want?' I ask her, prepared for anything. 'Is it the money? You can have it all if that's what it takes? I'll just leave with Cecilia and you'll be twenty grand richer. Everybody wins, right?'

I expect Victoria will eagerly accept my offer of all the money because I'm not really in any position to negotiate. Bizarrely, she doesn't look at all interested in what I've just said. Then I find out why.

'I don't want the money,' she tells me as Cecilia begins to cry in her arms. 'I want your baby.'

∧

TWENTY-THREE
ALICE

As soon as Tomlin told me he had a strong belief that Fern was in Cornwall, I ran home and immediately started packing. As far as I'm concerned, I'm ready to hit the road and start closing the distance between me and that woman and there is nothing anybody can say to try and stop me. But that's not preventing the man opposite me from trying.

'Just slow down. We still don't have a definite address yet!' Tomlin cries as I gather up my phone charger and chuck it into the rucksack that already has a spare change of clothes in it. I'm packing light, just essentials, which is why, once I've got my toothbrush, I think I'll be ready to go. Well, that and Evelyn and her bag of essentials of course, because I'm not leaving my little girl here with him, or her. Siobhan is still here, lingering awkwardly in my home and remaining totally oblivious to the fact that I know she was intimate with my boyfriend last night. But I couldn't give a damn about her or him. I just want to get down south as quickly as possible. Once I've got my bag and my baby in the car then I am going.

'This is ridiculous. What are you going to do? Just drive around and hope to spot her? Cornwall is a big place, you know?' Tomlin says. 'Just wait until we get a proper address, then we can go.'

'No, every second we waste is a second we risk Fern getting away again,' I cry as I zip up my bag then head for the bedroom door. Considering how I was on the verge of a nervous breakdown only a short time ago, I feel fully fit and raring to go now and it's amazing what adrenaline and a strong desire for revenge can do for a person's health.

I rush out of the bedroom, barging past Siobhan as I go, but she doesn't make an attempt at trying to get me to slow down. Instead, she suggests she comes with me.

'You might need help. Fern is dangerous. Let me come too,' she says.

The thought of being sat in a car for several hours with the woman who betrayed me is not quite a pleasant one. I think then about revealing what I saw and telling Siobhan to get lost but that will only delay my progress. I don't have time for an argument, I just need to get to my car, and as I get downstairs, I start packing things for Evelyn. I throw as many milk bottles as I can into her bag and figure I'll just pick up more on the way if I need to, but my speed is slowed by Tomlin and Siobhan who continue to get in my way.

'If you're really going to go then leave Evelyn here,' Tomlin suggests. 'We could leave her with a friend in the village. Audrey, perhaps. She'd be happy to help if she knew we were on our way to try and catch Fern.'

'No, she's coming with me,' I say, because I'm not leaving my baby with anyone, even if it would make the journey a lot easier. But I have no idea how long I'll be gone or what might happen, so Evelyn will have to come. But Tomlin is right about one thing. I shouldn't go by myself, which is why I say that he and Siobhan can come with me.

'Let's go get that bitch,' Siobhan says, clearly on board with this plan and, while she might be a bitch herself, for now, she can be an ally. But Tomlin is still unsure.

'I still think it's better if we wait and see what Ian finds in Cornwall,' he says. 'I only told you about this because you were so upset at the market. I wish I hadn't bothered now.'

'I was upset because that woman is still free. Now we know where she is, we can end this, once and for all,' I cry, excitement rising up inside me because I really do feel like the end could be in sight this time.

'I'm leaving and I'm going now,' I say to Tomlin as I push Evelyn and her pram towards the door while Siobhan grabs some bags and follows me. 'You can either come with us or you can stay here and potentially lose Fern again.'

I know that cutting remark will sting the proud detective, but also ensure he makes his decision quickly.

'Fine,' he says as he grabs his keys. 'But for the record, I think this is a bad idea and if we end up screwing this up and Fern gets away, this one will be on you.'

'She is not going to get away,' I say confidently as we leave the house and head for the car. 'I'll make sure of that.'

With the time for talking over, I ensure action takes precedent now and, once everything and everyone is in the car, I refuse Tomlin's suggestion that he drives and start the engine myself. Then I put my foot down and get us out of Arberness as quickly as possible, eager to join the motorway that will give me the quickest route all the way down to the south coast.

I can't wait to burn through these miles and get to where I'm going.

When I do, Fern is not going to believe her eyes.

TWENTY-FOUR

FERN

I stare at the woman holding my child and try to understand what she just said.

She doesn't want my money; she wants my baby.

But in what world does she think that is ever going to happen?

'Victoria, please, let's be sensible about this,' I say, holding out my hands towards my neighbour while she keeps her hands firmly on Cecilia, preventing me from taking my child and running from this flat, which is all I want to do.

'I am being sensible,' she replies coolly. 'I know you don't want to go to prison for the rest of your life, I'm sure you'll do anything to avoid that. This is what you have to do. Just let me leave with Cecilia and you will remain a free woman.'

'I'm not giving *you* my baby!' I cry and I step towards Victoria again, desperate to remove Cecilia from her clutches, but she just moves back and maintains her distance. I'm afraid of lunging too strongly at her in case she hurts the little life in her hands.

'You have no choice,' Victoria snaps back at me. 'Not if you want to keep yourself safe. And your daughter too for that matter.'

'You wouldn't hurt her,' I say, more out of desperate hope than of any certainty.

'I don't want to, but who knows what I am capable of if you push me,' Victoria says. 'You should know better than anyone that you should never judge a book by its cover. You have no idea what I have done before, just like everyone else in Cornwall has no idea they have a woman like you living amongst them. Stay back, Fern, or I'm warning you, this might not end well for any of us.'

Far too afraid to put that warning to the test, I do as Victoria says, keeping my distance while trying to figure a way out of this. But unless Victoria changes what she wants, I can't see one.

'Please, you know I can't give you my baby,' I say, my heart aching as I look at my girl and wish more than anything to be reunited with her. 'But I can give you money and lots of it. You can take it and start again somewhere new. I won't come after you. I don't care what you spend it on. Just please don't hurt my little girl.'

'I won't hurt her as long as you let me have her,' Victoria says, frighteningly. 'I've got an idea. Why don't you take the money and start again somewhere else? You're used to that, aren't you, so it shouldn't be too difficult for you. I meant it when I said I don't care about the money.'

'Only because you secretly wanted my child!' I cry. 'I never would have asked you for the favour if I'd known what you were capable of!'

'And I never would have been your friend if I'd known what you were capable of!' Victoria fires back. 'Deadly revenge plots. Murder. Framing an innocent person. Fraud. Do any of those things sound like something a great mother would do? Because you are not a great mother, Fern, far from it, and that is why Cecilia is better off with me than she is with you.'

I can't believe what I'm hearing. Despite my admittedly chequered past, there is no way she can seriously think that Cecilia belongs with her over me.

'Yes, I've done lots of things wrong,' I admit. 'But what you are trying to do here is way worse than any of that. You are trying to take a child from her mother and that is sick. She is my daughter, Victoria, not yours, so give her back to me or else.'

'Or else what? You'll hurt me like you hurt all those other people? Like you hurt your husband? That poor doctor made the biggest mistake of his life when he married you and he paid the price for it. But while you might have ruined his life, I'm not letting you ruin this little girl's. She deserves better than anything you can give her. She deserves a normal life, not a life on the run, and that is why she is staying with me.'

I can see now that Victoria is never going to change her mind, and that realisation is almost as frightening as when this whole nightmare started unfolding.

If I can't get her to give me Cecilia then what else can I do?

'What happened to you?' I ask, lowering my voice as I change tact slightly.

'Excuse me?' Victoria replies as Cecilia starts crying.

'What happened to make you into the kind of monster who would even try and do something like this? At least I had my reasons for what I did. My husband cheated on me, and I was upset and angry. I didn't just wake up one day and decide to do something terrible. It was a long process. Many months of feeling hurt and betrayed. Countless nights drowning in para-noia, shame and disgust. I never thought I was capable of being a woman who could hurt others, but I was forced into doing it by other people's actions.'

'You're blaming everything you have done on other people?'

Victoria asks me, looking appalled. 'Really? Like none of it was your fault?'

'No, that's not what I'm saying. What I am saying is that bad things happened to me and they led me to make bad decisions. What I want to know is what bad things happened to you to make you think that taking someone else's baby is okay?'

'None of your business.'

'It is my business when it's my baby you're trying to take!'

Victoria goes quiet at my outburst, as does Cecilia, who stops crying, no doubt stunned by the sound of her mother's voice being so loud.

'Whatever it is, Victoria, whatever happened to you, I'm sure it wasn't your fault. You have to see that this is not the right way to react to it. Please, just stop for a second and do the right thing. Don't make this worse for any of us.'

'Worse? How can things get any worse?' Victoria cries as she looks around. 'Look where I live. I'm on my own. I have nobody and nothing. I've never committed a crime yet this is my life, while look at you. You've done terrible things and yet you're the one blessed with a baby. It's not fair. I'd be a better parent than you. I know I'm a better human being than you!'

'So that's what this is all about? You're lonely? Well, I'm sorry about that, Victoria, but stealing a child is not the right way to go about changing that! I can help you make friends or meet a man or whatever it is you want. But I cannot give you my baby!'

My shock and fear is turning to anger now – I think Victoria can see that because, for the first time since this crazy scenario started unfolding, she looks a little surprised. Perhaps she thought I might back down in the face of her threatening to call the police, but if she thought that then she has been sadly mistaken.

'Just give Cecilia to me,' I say. 'Whatever you want to do

after that, whether it's to talk, call the police or just go back to whatever miserable life you had before, I don't care. Just give her back right now, or this will not end well for you.'

'What are you going to do?' Victoria says, attempting to match my display of strength by not backing down either.

'Let's just say that everyone who has ever crossed me has always come off much worse,' I remind Victoria, now deciding to use my past to my advantage. 'If you have done your research on me, and it sounds like you have, then you know exactly what happens to people who try and get in my way. So, this is your final warning. Give me back my daughter or I will not be responsible for my actions.'

I'm hoping Victoria will just concede and do as I wish. I should have known it wouldn't be that easy because nothing in my life ever is. Just like Drew when he couldn't stay away from Alice, or Rory when he told me he wanted to sleep with me in exchange for not going to the police, or Greg who secretly recorded my confession and tried to get away with it. Why do all the people who wrong me never realise that they are making a huge mistake until it is far too late?

Rushing at Victoria, I am prepared to have to try and catch Cecilia if she is dropped during the frantic exchange that is about to take place.

'Get away!' Victoria cries but I do no such thing, intent on getting back what is mine and to hell with the consequences.

As I try to get hold of Cecilia, Victoria tries to turn away from me, but I don't let her, as I get a grip on my daughter. Cecilia, clearly sensing the desperation of both the people surrounding her, is crying again and it's breaking my heart to see how afraid she is. But I know how much danger she is in if I don't get her away from this crazy woman, which is why I risk it all by making a very drastic move.

I push Victoria backwards as hard as I can and as she loses

her balance and falls. She loosens her grip on Cecilia, allowing me to take her from her before she hits the ground.

As I take hold of my baby, Victoria's head hits the edge of her coffee table and, after landing on the floor, she lies unresponsive on the carpet.

I wait to see if she is going to get up and try and get Cecilia back from me, but she doesn't move. I could be afraid that I have seriously injured her, if not killed her when I pushed her. But I don't have time to worry about that because now I have my baby back, I just want to get out of here and never see this woman again.

Running for the door, I know that if Victoria is dead then she can't come after me, nor can she go to the police and tell them who has been living next door to her. That would solve two very big problems for me, although if I have been responsible for another dead body, that would be a huge problem in itself. The police will eventually find her, and they will be asking around as to what happened, which is not what I need, because any police officers at my door could recognise me as the woman their colleagues have been looking for in other parts of the country. But if they do look into the dead body and discover that she only recently received a load of money from an account in the name of Drew Devlin, it won't take them long to figure out that I might have had something to do with both that transaction and the fact the woman who received the money is now dead. That's why I decide that, regardless of whether or not Victoria is dead or alive, I am going to get back to my flat and pack my things and then I am going to get the hell out of this place.

I wasn't planning on leaving Cornwall and hoped to build a real life for me and my daughter here, but once again, things have changed fast. At least I haven't lost my ability to adapt and overcome problems. I'm a survival specialist and I'm going to need all those skills once again.

As I return to my flat and put Cecilia down in her crib before beginning to pack my clothes, I have the horrible feeling that, for some reason, this time, my luck is about to run out.

I don't know why, but I can just sense it.

This trouble is not over.

TWENTY-FIVE

ALICE

I've been driving for two hours now, the dial on the speedometer constantly just above the regulated speed limits on the motorways I'm zooming along, the distance between my car and Cornwall growing ever smaller by the second. However, despite making good progress, it's never going to be fast enough for me because I want to be there yesterday. I'm also feeling slowed by the passengers in my car. Siobhan is sitting in the front beside me while Tomlin is in the back next to Evelyn's car seat, and while I am eager to keep going, both of them are keen to stop soon.

'Evelyn is due a feed and a change,' Tomlin keeps telling me, no matter how much I try to ignore him and just focus on the road ahead.

'There's a service station coming up in five miles,' Siobhan adds unhelpfully, because I have no intention of stopping. Parking this car will not get me to Fern quicker, so why should I stop? Unfortunately, as any driver knows, it's extremely difficult to have a comfortable journey when your passengers are unsettled and, when Evelyn starts crying, clearly hungry and in need of a break from her car seat, I realise I'm fighting a losing battle.

We're going to have to stop.

But only for a short time.

'Let's make this quick,' I say as I indicate to come off the motorway and drive us towards the service station.

Evelyn's crying grows louder as I look for a place to park amongst all the other vehicles owned by motorists who also felt like they needed some respite from the road. Maybe it will do me some good to get out of this car for a minute, if only to have a break from the sound of crying. I finally find a space, pulling up beside a large SUV, inside of which three kids jump out, closely followed by their frazzled looking parents.

'I'll do the feed,' Tomlin says as he pulls an empty milk bottle and some ready-made formula from the large bag by his feet in the back of the car, before getting Evelyn into position on his lap. I could offer to help him, but I prefer to take the opportunity to stretch my legs beside the car, with Siobhan doing the same thing.

It doesn't take long to feed Evelyn because she is well beyond being hungry and always drains the milk bottles faster when that is the case. Once that's done, Tomlin is ready for the next task.

'Let's take her inside and change her there,' Tomlin says as he joins us outside the car.

'Can't we just do it here?' I protest. 'It'll take too long if we get the pram out and there's probably a thousand other babies inside there being changed. We don't have time for big queues.'

'I'm not changing her in the car. She needs a change of scene, as do I. We'll just have half an hour. We can afford that.'

The thought of delaying this journey by thirty minutes is not a pleasant one, but there's little I can do barring getting in this car and driving away from here without any of my passengers in it. That thought is actually a tempting one, because I'm still harbouring the knowledge of what Tomlin and Siobhan did behind my back, which has made a tense car journey even tenser as we travelled south from Arberness. I'm constantly having to grit my teeth as Tomlin tries to tell me what is best for me and my baby, while Siobhan keeps reminding me how much she is on my side and can't wait to help me get justice for what Fern did to me. They are not acting like two people who stabbed me in the back but I know they are capable of it, which is why I am not going to let either of them get away with it.

I just need to pick my moment and that will be a time when it isn't going to stop me getting to Fern.

Like most things in life that are attempted after having a child, which take more time and are more arduous, that is the case with this car journey as the four of us enter the service station, looking to get Evelyn's nappy changed and relieve ourselves too. Once inside the service station, I see lines of people queuing at various fast food places, all of them looking to fuel their bodies after presumably fuelling their cars as well. As I suspected, I also see plenty of parents taking their babies into the restrooms and the queues there are almost as long and slow-moving as the queues for the food.

'I'll be right back,' Tomlin says as he takes Evelyn to join the queue and that leaves me and Siobhan to go and get some food.

'I fancy a sandwich,' she says to me before suggesting we check out the shop to our left that looks like it sells sandwiches, amongst many other products, ranging from big packets of crisps to tempting chocolate bars and colourful cans of fizzy drinks. But they sell something else too and, as we enter the shop, we both see the rows of magazines on display to the right of the checkouts. Several headlines are vying for a potential reader's attention but it's the one on the front cover in the middle of the rack that wins the battle for me. It's carrying a headline that relates directly to me and my reason for being on the road today.

I went to school with the deadly Doctor's Widow

The lettering is bright yellow on the front cover of the trashy real-life gossip magazine, and while Siobhan hasn't noticed it herself, she does see it when I reach out and pick the magazine off the shelf.

Staring at the cover, I see there is a photo of Fern on there, alongside another woman who seems to be the one who has sold her story to this fairly unreputable publication.

'People will cash in on anything,' Siobhan comments as she sees me turning the pages to find the story. 'Did I tell you a journalist offered me two thousand pounds to talk about what it was like being in prison with you? I told him to get lost because I valued my friendship with you far more than making a bit of easy money.'

I don't say anything to Siobhan, not just because I'm looking at the magazine but because I know she clearly doesn't value our friendship enough to keep her hands off my man. Then I find the article I'm looking for and, as I quickly read it, I find out the story is about one of Fern's old classmates from a school in Manchester who is talking all about what the wanted woman was like as a child and pupil.

> I think her favourite subject was maths. She used to sit behind me in English, but she didn't answer many questions. I know she liked geography too because she once did a presentation on the continents of the world. I had no idea when I knew her that she would go on to marry a doctor and I certainly had no idea she would break the law. It's shocking to think what she became, and I just hope the police can catch her before she causes any more harm to an innocent person.

Alongside the columns of words are a few more photos and Drew is in one of them, the handsome doctor pictured on holiday somewhere warm and sunny and totally oblivious to the grim fate that awaited him in his future. There is also a photo of me in here, one taken as I left prison and I know it was then because I look awful in the photo. There is a caption beneath it.

The Doctor's Mistress: Alice Richardson was framed by Fern and sentenced for murder before the true story came out.

I wonder if the editor of this magazine was supposed to ask for my permission before they used my photo but it's too late for that now, nor can I say I really care because it's not as if this is the first time my image has been displayed for public consumption in relation to this story.

I close the magazine without reading the full article because I can get the gist of it.

I toss it back onto the shelf and go in search of what I came in here for, which is some food. Siobhan can obviously tell that I am upset by the article because she tries to console me, telling me that this will be over soon and, when it is, all the stories that are printed will be about how Fern got her comeuppance and I ended up being the hero of the story.

Maybe Siobhan is right. I certainly hope she is. But as she goes on and on about how everything is going to work out well for me in the end, I can't quite see how that is possible if I am stuck with her and Tomlin for the rest of this trip. Being around one liar might be tolerable, but not two, which is why I have an idea of how to get rid of one of them.

We buy our food and wait for Tomlin to return from the restrooms with Evelyn. Then the four of us make our way back to the car. But as I get there and Tomlin begins the often tricky process of switching Evelyn from the pram to the car seat, I ask Siobhan if she could do me a favour.

'I should have got a coffee,' I say, faking a yawn to enforce just how much I could do with a caffeine hit right about now. 'Do you think you could go back and get me one? Sorry.'

'No problem at all,' Siobhan replies, which I knew she

would because she's made it clear ever since we set off from Arberness that she is here to help me.

'I should probably get one too actually,' she says before checking in with Tomlin if he would like one as well.

He says yes and as I go to give him some help with Evelyn, Siobhan walks back to join the queues of people inside the service station.

'I thought you were eager to get back on the road,' Tomlin says to me, probably wondering why I've just added another delay to our journey.

'I am,' I say as the pair of us get into the car, and I guess my boyfriend is still under the false assumption that we are going to wait for the woman who has gone to get us coffee. But that's not what I'm planning to do. As I start the engine, Tomlin asks me what I am doing.

'I'm putting some distance between us and that woman you kissed last night,' I say coolly before driving away and, funnily enough, Tomlin doesn't quite know what to say to that.

Once he has got over the shock of me calling him out on what he did last night with my so-called friend, he tells me to stop because we can't just leave her here in the middle of nowhere. But there's no way I'm listening to him and, very soon, I'm back on the motorway and zooming away from Siobhan at seventy miles per hour.

Do I feel bad for leaving her behind? Not at all. She betrayed me, so I'm only getting my own back. Now she is already in my rear-view mirror, I can turn my attentions back to the other woman who messed with me.

I've just taken care of one lying bitch.

Now it's time to take care of another.

TWENTY-SIX

FERN

I can't believe this is happening again. Not only am I having to go back on the run but I'm also having to process the fact that I may have just hurt another person.

As I pack my things, I keep telling myself that I had no choice. Victoria was trying to take my child. What else is a mother supposed to do in that situation other than fight back? I didn't mean to hurt her, but I had to do something to get my baby back. Cecilia is currently in her crib, but she must be able to sense that something is wrong because she is crying loudly, and that noise is only adding to the stressful situation I find myself in.

As I throw my things into my suitcase, I can't help but wonder if I can no longer keep passing off all the things I do as being other people's fault. So far, the only reason I've been able to lay my head down on my pillow at night and get some sleep is because I've told myself that other people forced me into doing bad things. But what if there comes a point when I have to take full responsibility for my actions? And acknowledge that it can't be a coincidence – everywhere I go, I leave a trail of death and destruction.

What if I'm the problem?

What if I'm as bad as the newspapers say I am?

Worst of all, what if Cecilia is actually better off without me?

Perhaps the only thing worse than losing your child is realising they might actually have a better life without you. As I stop packing and stare at my screaming baby, I know that she doesn't deserve any of this. Perhaps the best thing for me to do now is quit running and hand myself into the police. Cecilia would be taken into care and, eventually, a new family would be found for her to go and live with. She could have a normal upbringing then, rather than the mess of a life she would have if she stayed with me. She could be raised in a calm and safe environment where she could flourish, rather than whatever unpredictable and dangerous places she would end up in with me.

While my bond with my girl seems unbreakable, what if actually breaking it would be the best way for her to have a chance of thriving in adulthood?

I know there will come a time when she learns about who her mother really was and what she did but, at least if there is some separation between us by then, it might not have such a profound impact on her. She might have better role models in her life by then who could have shown her the difference between right and wrong and the legal ways to deal with problems, rather than all the illegal ways I chose to deal with mine. Maybe one day, she could come and visit me in prison, and while it would be brutal for the pair of us, at least she would see that I had owned up to my mistakes and was facing the consequences of them rather than continuing to run from them.

The problem is, while all that sounds good in theory, it is going to be much harder, if not impossible, for me to willingly walk away from my daughter and into a prison cell. Who knows, it may even have an adverse effect on Cecilia. She might feel abandoned by the one woman who was supposed to be with her forever, and that could screw up her mentality in adulthood far more than just living a nomadic and impoverished existence with me as she grows. At least if I stick with her, no matter what happens in the future, she can never accuse me of leaving her and not loving her. Selfishly, choosing that second course of action also helps keep me out of prison, for a while at least, so it's easier for me to feel like that is the best way to go.

So that's what I'll do.

I'll keep running with Cecilia by my side and I won't stop fighting for us until there's nothing left to fight for.

Deciding that I've packed enough of my things, I am just about to start on Cecilia's stuff when I realise the cause of her screaming may simply be that she is hungry. She is overdue a feed and while I really don't have time for stopping, it's not going to be easy maintaining a low profile as I attempt to leave this village if I'm carrying a crying child around with me. That's why I decide to feed her now, because who knows when I'll get the chance to do it next?

Picking her up from her crib, I put her on my left breast, and she instantly calms, which gives me a chance to hear myself think. Telling myself to stay calm, I feel like I can get out of this messy situation. Once this feed is done, I'll pack Cecilia's things and then we'll leave in the direction of the bus station. Once there, I'll take the first bus out of this village and get as far away as I can. I'll keep moving for a few days, zigzagging around so there's not much of a trail for anybody to follow before I'll hopefully find somewhere I feel like I can start again with Cecilia. Depending on whether or not the police are interested in Victoria's missing neighbour will determine whether or not I can keep using my new persona or if I'll have to ditch my fake IDs and figure out another way, but I'll cross that bridge when I come to it. For now, it's just about getting away from here before people start knocking on Victoria's door and discovering that something terrible happened.

Knowing that she lives alone, it could be a while until somebody realises something is wrong with her. Thinking about it, it will probably be our landlord, Nigel, who is the first to figure it out. That's because he'll come calling when rent is due, as he always does, and when Victoria fails to answer the door, he'll just let himself in with the spare keys he has for all his properties. Then he'll find the body and sound the alarm and, seeing as how he'll quickly find out that I've vanished, he will probably tell the police I might have had something to do with it.

Cecilia finishes feeding, which means there is no more time for paranoid thoughts about the future. Instead, it's time to take action and I put her in her pram before going in search of her bag with her bibs, nappies and dummies in.

But it's not here.

Searching everywhere, I can't understand where it could be until it dawns on me.

It must be at Victoria's.

She would have had it when she was looking after Cecilia and that means it must be in her flat somewhere now. I obviously wasn't collected enough to look around and make sure I wasn't leaving anything behind when I ran for the door with my baby in my arms seconds after snatching her from that crazy woman. But that means I've left evidence of myself being there in her flat beside her body and that will only make it easier for any police officers to connect me to that scene.

I know what I need to do.

I need to go and retrieve that bag.

Wishing I could do anything other than return to that place I was so glad to escape from only a short time ago, I think about just risking it and leaving the bag. I have the money to buy replacement things for Cecilia and is it really worth me returning to the scene of the crime? But then I think about how, if I leave the bag, it makes it very obvious that I was there with my baby. Along with the fact that my landlord will tell the police that I'm missing, it's a slam dunk as far as the investigation into who must have hurt Victoria goes.

Not willing to make things that easy for the next bunch of police officers who will soon be on my tail, I make sure Cecilia is safe enough to be left in her pram for a few minutes before going out the back door of my flat. Then I hop over the wall between mine and Victoria's place and try her back door, which thankfully opens. If not, I might have had to break in but at least that would have given the police something else to look at and possibly distract them.

Cautiously stepping inside, I look around and instantly see Cecilia's bag sitting on the kitchen table. But just before I can go and pick it up, I look down to where I left Victoria when I pushed her over and ran out of here.

But she's no longer there.

TWENTY-SEVEN

ALICE

After I drove us away from the service station, Tomlin spent the first five minutes of the journey telling me that it was unfair to leave Siobhan behind and that I should go back and get her. He then spent the next five minutes apologising to me about what he did with her, telling me that it was just a stupid mistake, meant nothing and it would never have happened again. You know, all the usual nonsense a cheating liar comes out with when they have been caught. After ignoring both the pleas and the apology, he moved onto telling me to slow down because I've been zooming along this motorway above the speed limit and he thinks it's unsafe, even though the traffic is light, and the driving conditions are good. But just like everything else, I have been ignoring him because I'm making good time now in getting to Cornwall. Every second that I go faster is a second nearer to me hopefully finding Fern.

After giving up on talking to me and going quiet in the back seat for a little while, Tomlin has taken to watching Evelyn sleeping in her car seat. Whenever I glance up and see them in my rear-view mirror, I am reminded of how good he is with her. The pang of pain I feel in my heart about being mad at him over what he has done also reminds me that I still haven't fully decided if I am going to end things with him or not. He hasn't come out and asked me that question himself yet, probably because he is afraid of the answer, but he might also just be grateful that he hasn't been left stranded at the service station like the other love rat has.

After travelling on in silence for a little longer, I'm interrupted by the voice from the satnav when it tells me that I am within an hour of my destination now. That destination is a generic part of Cornwall, as centrally located as I could select because, at present, I still don't know exactly whereabouts in that county Fern is. At least I'll be in the right part of the country, soon by the looks of it, and it's amazing how quickly you can get somewhere when you play fast and loose with the accelerator pedal, although I'm forced to drop my speed a little when I see a police car joining the motorway up ahead.

Almost at the same time as I slow down, Tomlin's phone starts ringing and, when I ask him who is calling, he tells me it's Ian, the man who has so far tracked Fern down to Cornwall.

He must have an update for us.

'Hey,' Tomlin says as he answers, keeping his voice low so as not to disturb the resting Evelyn beside him. But while I understand the need for being quiet, I wish he would put the call on loudspeaker so I could hear what information is being passed on from the other end of the line. As it is, I have to be patient as Tomlin listens, but my desire to know what is going on only increases when I see Tomlin look surprised before he asks a strange question.

'What? Are you sure?'

'What's happening?' I ask him, my eyes flitting between the road and the rear-view mirror, but Tomlin just raises a hand for me to be quiet as he keeps on listening. That's frustrating but there's not much I can do other than keep driving, so I do that until finally the call ends with Tomlin telling the man at the other end of the line that we will be with him very soon and to keep watching her until then.

That sounds to me like he has found her!

'What is it? Does he have her address?' I ask, unbridled excitement threatening to make me jerk the steering wheel and cause the car to shift too far one way or the other.

'He's found her,' Tomlin says calmly, but while he might be trying to play it cool, he also can't contain all his excitement and a smile curls at the edges of his lips.

'That's great! Where is she?' I ask him, quickly taking one hand off the wheel and poising my finger to type a new address into the satnav. But Tomlin isn't quite as quick to answer me.

'What are you doing? What did he say?' I cry, desperate to know and not caring if the volume of my voice wakes Evelyn up.

'He has her address,' Tomlin confirms. 'He's outside her place right now. It's a small flat. But there's something you need to know.'

'What?'

'She's not alone.'

'What do you mean?'

'She has a baby with her.'

'What?'

I'm trying to process what I just heard, but it doesn't make any sense.

Fern has a baby with her?

'What baby?'

'I don't know, but Ian is adamant she has a child. Fern, or Teresa Brown as she is going by, is registered at a doctor's in Bowey, but there is an infant registered with her too. Cecilia Brown. Ian has gone to her address and has told me he has seen Fern going into her property recently with a baby in her arms, who appears to be aged around three months old.

'Whose baby is that?' I cry, stunned at this unexpected twist because I'd been imagining Fern living a rotten life all by herself, yet apparently she has a child with her.

'It's hers,' Tomlin says, though he seems as unsure about that as I am.

'I don't understand. Who is the father?' I ask him and he shakes his head before suddenly looking like he might have an answer.

'Who?' I ask him again.

'It could be Greg's,' he replies quietly.

I instantly think of the man who was trying to get me out of prison, the old friend of Drew's who got close to Fern and helped expose her, but not without giving up his life in the process.

'He told me that he was sleeping with her when he came to see me at the police station in Carlisle,' Tomlin goes on. 'I warned him about that, but he said it was the only way he could maintain the illusion of being her boyfriend. Maybe she got pregnant just before she killed him.'

It's my turn to shake my head and, once again, nothing is ever as it seems when it comes to Fern.

But there is an alternative to Greg being the father.

'What if it's Drew's baby?' I say, cold to the idea that the deceased doctor might have fathered two babies before he passed away. But given that Fern's baby is younger than mine, I doubt it could be. I conceived just before Drew met his demise, so Tomlin must be right. The baby is Greg's.

Two children growing up without their fathers.

This rotten situation Fern and I are in just gets worse.

'Do you think we should pause and think about this,' Tomlin asks me then.

'What?'

'Well, now we know she has a baby, it changes things.'

'No, it doesn't! She is still a killer, and she still deserves to go to prison.'

'Yes, but what about the baby?'

'What about it? Getting that baby away from her is the best thing for that child.'

Tomlin looks unsure but I'm not slowing down. I just need the address.

'Tell me where she is,' I say, but Tomlin is still reluctant.

'Now we have her, I really think this is where we should let the police take over,' he says. 'We can be there, and we can watch her get arrested, but we've done as much as we can. It's time to finish this and the safest way to do that is calling for back up.'

'No, you know how important this is to me. I have to be the one to do it. Don't deny me that.'

'But think of her baby. Think of your baby. What might happen if you just storm in there? It's too unpredictable.'

'Just give me the damn address and I'll worry about it when I get there,' I say and Tomlin very reluctantly does as I ask, possibly because it's not good to have an angry, frustrated woman at the wheel at these speeds. I calm down quickly once he has given me the address, although I certainly don't slow down.

Not now I know exactly where Fern is.

I'll be there very soon.

And there's nothing she can do about it.

TWENTY-EIGHT

FERN

'No, this can't be happening,' I say to myself for what must be the fourth or fifth time since I discovered Victoria was not lying on the floor where I left her.

In one way, it's good news, because it means I didn't kill her like I feared.

In another way, it's terrifying, because I have no idea where the woman who hates me is now.

After what unfolded between us, Victoria must be angry and intent on getting revenge and that is why, after I have made sure that I have Cecilia's bag, I run out the back door and go over the wall to return to my flat, intent on just grabbing everything I am taking with me and getting out of here before Victoria can get her own back on me for pushing her over and denying her the chance to take my baby. Entering my flat, I freeze because there is somebody standing beside Cecilia's pram.

Thankfully, it's not Victoria.

But it is still a problem.

'What's going on here then?' Nigel asks me and I stay still as

I stare at my landlord and wonder why my bad luck seems to be continuing today.

'What are you doing here?' I ask him. 'You can't just come inside!'

'I knocked twice on the door, but there was no answer,' he tells me. 'I've come to fix the tap, so I let myself in. I am within my rights to do that when I'm here to maintain the property.'

Now he has explained himself, I am aware that Nigel has a right to enter my home when he is here to fix something I have reported as being broken, though I'm sure there should be twenty-four hours' notice given, although in this case, I guess he figured the sooner the tap is fixed, the better. I also figure that he must have been knocking while I was next door getting the bag from Victoria's flat. However, it's still very unfortunate, because I was hoping to be running out the door. Now he's here, I'm stuck. Worse than that, he can easily see that I'm planning on leaving and never coming back.

'Are you going somewhere?' he asks me, but it's not really a tough question because with all my bags packed and ready to go, it's clear that I am.

'Erm, yeah,' I say, before thinking of something that sounds less dramatic than telling him that I'm fleeing this village. 'I'm just going to stay with a friend up north for a few days.'

'Staying with a friend for a few days?' Nigel repeats back to me before stepping back and looking into the bedroom. 'Do you usually take everything with you when you go away for a few days?'

'Well, I don't have much stuff,' I reply. 'And I'm not taking everything.'

'It looks like you are. There's nothing left here.'

'Like I said, I'll be back in a few days. But I have a bus to catch now, so I better be going.'

I push the pram towards the door with one hand while carrying my suitcase in the other, with Cecilia's bag over my shoulder. Before I can get out, Nigel steps in front of me and, while I had been hoping he'd just believe my story about visiting a friend and allow me to go, when has my life ever been that easy?

'Just hang on a minute,' he says to me, blocking my escape route. 'You wouldn't be leaving without telling me, would you?'

'Leaving? No, I'm just going away for a few days like I said. I'll be back soon.'

Nigel just smirks and shakes his head. 'If there's one thing I've got experience of since becoming a landlord, it's having tenants who try to sneak away without telling me, especially when they still have outstanding debts to pay.'

'I don't have any outstanding debts.'

'Don't you?' Nigel says. 'Next month's rent is due soon.'

'It's not due until next Friday.'

'But if you're leaving, I won't have time to find a new tenant before then, which means I won't be getting any money on Friday, will I? You're supposed to give me thirty days' notice if you intend to leave.'

'I'm not leaving!'

I try again, but it's in vain and Nigel knows it.

'What's the matter?' he asks me. 'You're all flustered. What's going on? You can tell me.'

I definitely cannot tell him, so I need another way of getting him to move out the way.

'Fine, I am leaving. But I can give you your money. It's not a problem,' I say, and I quickly drop my suitcase down before reaching into my pockets and pulling out the wedge of cash Victoria withdrew from the bank earlier.

Pulling out twenty pound notes, I count out how much I owe Nigel before holding it out for him to take. But surprisingly, he doesn't grab the cash and step aside.

'Woah, somebody has come to into a bit of money, haven't they?' he says, staring at all the bank notes in my hand and I realise now that it was probably a bad idea to take all of it out in front of him. 'Where did you get all that from?'

'None of your business,' I reply. 'Do you want your money or not?'

'It depends where that money came from and whether or not it's linked to anything illegal.'

'It's not illegal. It's my money.'

'You really expect me to believe that a woman like you who has chosen to live here would suddenly have that much cash on her?' Nigel says, shaking his head. 'I know you're poor, just like everybody else who rents a flat around here. That's why rent is so cheap. So, I'll ask you again. Where did you get that money from?'

Every second I'm stood here having this conversation is another second when Victoria could be on her way to the police station to tell them who I am, so I do not have time for this.

'Please, just take the money and let me leave,' I beg. 'I just want to go.'

'Why?'

'Why does it matter?'

'Because I think you're hiding something, and I want to know what it is. I have a right considering you are my tenant.'

'Not anymore. I'm your ex-tenant.'

'You know, I could just call the police and have them come here and ask you.'

'The police? Why would you call them?'

'Because I suspect one of my tenants has broken the law,' he says, almost in a relaxed manner, as if he is fully in control here, which he just might be.

'I haven't broken the law,' I say desperately.

'Then tell me where the money came from because I know you don't have a job.'

'Just take it. Please,' I try one more time and I thrust the money I owe him into his chest.

He does take it from me, which gives me hope that he is about to step aside. But he doesn't. Instead, he looks me up and down, making me feel very uncomfortable as his eyes move over me.

'You know, I've always liked you,' he says, and my body turns cold as he speaks. 'What do you say that, in exchange for me not making a big deal out of this and letting you leave shortly, we go into the bedroom for a little while. Call it a proper goodbye between two friends.'

That suggestion makes me feel sick and I let Nigel know it.

'You're disgusting,' I say. 'Get out of my way!'

I push forward to the door then, using the pram as a tool to hopefully help me get there, and it does work in so much as it gets Nigel to move before the pram slams into his leg. That allows me to open the door and I'm just about to get out when he puts a hand over my mouth and drags me back inside.

After pushing me to the floor beside the pram, Nigel slams the door shut again before turning to face me. For a horrifying moment, I feel like I am about to be attacked right here with my daughter in the same room. It certainly looks like that is about to happen as Nigel leers over me and starts to reach for his belt buckle.

But then there is a knock at the door and the surprise of it catches us both off guard. Fortunately, I react much quicker to it than him and, snatching Cecilia from her pram, I run with her to the back door, leaving all my luggage behind but not caring about that, only that the pair of us can get away.

'Hey, come back here!' Nigel calls after me but I don't slow down. Once I'm out the back door, I race through the gate that leads into the alleyway and continue sprinting for as long as I am confident Nigel is not behind me.

When I finally turn back and look, I don't see him, so I pause to catch my breath. Even though I don't have any of my clothes, nor any of Cecilia's things, I am just grateful that we both escaped that place.

I still have most of the money on me too, barring what I gave to Nigel, so I have the funds to get myself out of here and set off in the direction of the nearest taxi rank. Forget public transport. I just need to get away from here as quickly as I can because between Victoria, Nigel and potentially the police too, I have enough people who would love to catch up with me and I am already running on borrowed time.

Jogging towards the promenade, I know there are always plenty of taxis at the other end of it, so I should be in a cab and on my way out of here in the next five minutes or so.

I'm on the run again, in all senses of the word.

TWENTY-NINE

ALICE

We've already passed a road sign welcoming us to Cornwall. As a sign for Bowey comes into view, I know we are almost there now. As we draw nearer, Tomlin is becoming more vocal on the back seat, wanting to know exactly what my plan is when we get to Fern's flat, although I have complete tunnel vision at this time and am only focused on getting to where I need to be as quickly as possible. Annoyingly, the traffic has got heavier as we have got nearer. With the motorways having given way to narrower roads, the route is more congested, and I'm forced into slowing down. Having to keep touching the brake pedal is not doing anything to ease the nerves I am feeling, but I make sure not to show Tomlin that I am getting anxious. Any sign of weakness from me now will only make him question me further.

But his questions have to stop when his phone rings again, and when he answers I make sure to tell him to put the call on loudspeaker this time so I can listen in as well. He does that, either because I was firm when I told him to do so or because Evelyn is already awake in her car seat, so any extra volume won't disturb her much now. With the call connected, I can hear Ian at the other end of the line.

'Fern's on the move,' he tells us. 'She has left her flat with the baby and it looks like she's in a rush to get somewhere.'

'Where's she going?' Tomlin asks as I silently curse the car in front of me and wish I could drive through them – I'm not liking what I'm hearing. I don't want to know about Fern moving around because, if she's moving, she will be harder to catch.

'I'm not sure, but I'm following her,' Ian replies. 'There's something else.'

'What?' I snap, my loud voice from the front of the car easily heard down the phone. Tomlin has to quickly let Ian know that I'm listening in too.

'There was an incident at Fern's flat,' Ian tells us. 'A man entered her home a short time ago and I kept watch. Nothing happened until the door opened again and it appeared that Fern was trying to get away from the man. But he dragged her back inside and slammed the door.'

Tomlin and I make eye contact in the rear-view mirror as we process this information.

'Who was it?' Tomlin asks, but Ian has no idea.

'I'm not sure but he'd let himself into the flat with a key so it could have been a boyfriend, or maybe a landlord. I don't know, but it was clear that something bad was happening. Fern was troubled, hence why I intervened.'

'You intervened?' I cry.

'Yes, from my point of view and the glimpse into the flat I got when Fern was dragged back inside after almost leaving, it looked like a potential assault was imminent. I was not willing to stand by and do nothing with a woman and child possibly in harm's way, so I approached the flat and knocked on the door in an attempt to disturb the man.'

'What? You've broken your cover!' I cry, wondering why Ian would be so stupid as to do such a thing as approach Fern, because then isn't it obvious that he's been watching her? And if she knows she's been watched, she'll know someone is onto her.

'No, I haven't because Fern didn't see me,' Ian said. 'Even if she had, I would have just passed myself off as a salesman. Anyway, when the door was eventually opened, the man inside looked flustered and angrily asked who I was. I could see past him and saw that Fern and the baby were no longer inside, so I immediately left and went around the rear of the property, which is where I saw Fern making her escape.'

'So where is she now?' I ask as I am forced to hit the brakes again in this procession of slow-moving vehicles, luggage piled high inside their cars and bicycles fixed to the top of them, the occupants all clearly coming here for a holiday. *Damn these tourists.*

'She's making her way along the promenade,' Ian tells us and, as he says that, I see a sign for that promenade come into view and, mercifully, it seems to be in a different direction to where most of the cars in front of me are going.

'Got it! We're almost there!' I shout as I turn off and, when I do, the sea comes into view in the distance. It looks lovely and blue but I'm not here to take photos. I'm here for *her* and, by the sounds of it, I am almost right on top of her.

As Ian tries to describe which part of the promenade Fern is currently on, I see said promenade come into view – I also see dozens of people strolling along the seafront and enjoying the view. This makes it harder for me to spot the person I am looking for but, with Ian helping us, we do stand more of a chance of finding Fern amongst this busy scene. However, things take a turn for the worst when Ian suddenly says he has momentarily lost her in the crowd.

'What do you mean you've lost her!' I cry, anguished and afraid because I haven't come this far to not get what I want. The woman who put me in prison is around here somewhere and she has no idea that I am so close. My imminent revenge is simply too delicious a thought to give up now, which is why I decide to just park the car and abandon it, figuring it will be easier to find Fern if I am amongst the crowd rather than simply driving alongside the edge of it.

'What are you doing?' Tomlin cries as I bring the car to a stop by the roadside.

'I'm finding her!' I say, no longer wishing to put my fate in the hands of Ian, who already seems to have lost her.

'Just wait! You can't park here!' Tomlin cries, but while he might have already looked for any signs that advise motorists on where they can and cannot stop, I don't give a damn about that. I only want to find the woman I came here for.

And then I see her.

She's about fifty metres or so ahead of my car, weaving in and out of the pedestrians, a baby in her arms and a troubled look on her face. Best of all, she is heading in my direction, and I know that this is the moment I have been waiting for.

'There she is!' I cry, pointing through my windscreen before unbuckling my seatbelt and opening my door.

'Alice! Slow down!' Tomlin tries, but there's not a single thing that him or anybody else could say to slow me down now. As I run into the crowd, I am bearing down on Fern and her baby and know this is about to be over.

'Got you!' I cry as I reach out and grab Fern's arm. She instantly tenses up and stops walking, looking up at me with fear on her face before that expression is quickly replaced by one of total shock.

'It's over, bitch! Time to pay for everything you have done,' I say, finally uttering the words I have long since dreamt about saying – you best believe it feels as good as I imagined it would. 'You're going to prison and this time you will not get out of it!'

Within a split second, Fern's shock has worn off and she tries to release herself from my grip, pulling away while holding on tightly to the baby in her arms. But I'm not letting her go and am not going to be persuaded into going easier on her just because she is with a child. Of course, I don't want to hurt her baby, but I am not risking losing her in this crowd either.

'This woman is a murderer!' I cry, instantly getting the attention of the pedestrians beside us. Very quickly, a circle forms around us as people give us space while wondering what is disturbing the peace in this usually calm place.

'Get off me!' Fern tries. Maybe it's because she is still shocked, or maybe she is weaker and less fearsome now she has another life to look after, but she is not the adversary I thought she would be when I finally caught up with her. I keep hold of her easily and, despite everything she has done, it seems like she is the one who is afraid of me. As she well should be, because there isn't much I won't do to keep this woman from escaping. Now I have been the one to stop her, all I need is the police to get here. That's why I turn to look for Tomlin because he can help me by calling for them, or he can ask Ian to do it. Whatever. The point is that I'm finally ready to enlist the help of others and, right on cue, Tomlin appears, looking almost as worried as Fern does.

When he reaches me he quickly examines Fern to make sure she doesn't pose a threat to me, while also checking that I'm not doing something stupid like being unnecessarily violent towards her, because that would only see me get in trouble with the police too. But everything is under control, or at least I think it is until I look past Tomlin and see something troubling.

The car door beside Evelyn's seat is open but, as far as I can tell, she is not with Tomlin.

'Where's Evelyn?' I say, alerting him to the fact that, in all the chaos, both of us appear to have become too distracted as to keep watch on my little girl. As he looks back at the car, I tell him to keep an eye on Fern while I go to get her.

Tomlin quickly takes hold of Fern's arm and, while she continues to protest and try to wriggle free, I run back to the car because there are a lot of people around and it won't be wise to leave Evelyn for any longer than we already have done.

But then I look inside the car and, when I do, I get as big a shock as Fern just got when I caught her.

That's because my baby is not there.

THIRTY

FERN

No, this can't be happening.

How has this happened?

What the hell am I going to do now?

'Get off me!' I try again, urging the detective who has a strong grip on me to let me go. He and Alice have obviously been working together to track me down and now they have done it, though I have no idea how.

I thought I had been so careful, but they've outsmarted me.

'Get off!' I try again, although I get the sinking feeling there is absolutely nothing that can happen now that will cause him to do such a thing.

Or so I thought.

It's a second later when Alice, having briefly left us to return to her car, lets out the most horrifying cry of pain. As awful as it is, I also recognise it, because it's very similar to a reaction I produced not so long ago.

When she actually starts saying words again, I realise exactly the same thing that happened to me earlier today is happening to the doctor's mistress.

'Where is my baby?' Alice cries at the top of her voice,

causing everyone on this promenade to turn and look at her. Despite the huge problem I am currently facing, it seems somebody here is worse off than me.

'What's going on?' I ask Tomlin as I feel his grip lessen slightly on me, but I'm not quite thinking about running yet because I'm trying to understand this situation.

Tomlin looks just as confused as me and things only get more confusing when a man joins us, though he seems to know the detective.

'Is everything okay?' he asks Tomlin before he looks at me, then I wonder just how big this operation to find me has actually been and how many people it involves. Am I surrounded by a bunch of plain-clothed police officers? If so, there isn't much I can do even if I break away from the man holding onto me.

But Tomlin's grip continues to loosen as Alice cries out for help. When she starts running down the promenade, calling out for her baby before dropping to her knees and letting out a howl of pain, he lets go of me entirely and runs towards the stricken woman.

Suddenly free, I think about running but I am unable to tear my eyes away from Alice and the state of grief she is clearly in. Having briefly lost Cecilia earlier, I know exactly what she is going through now, which is why it is impossible for me to be so uncaring, even if this woman came here to put me behind bars.

The man who just joined us quickly takes hold of me as if he thinks I am about to run, but I tell him I'll not going anywhere and surprise him by pulling away before rushing over to Alice and Tomlin. The detective who messed up my husband's murder investigation so spectacularly is now crouching beside the kneeling Alice and trying to help her, but the only thing that can improve this situation is if they find the missing child.

How is that possible in such a busy place?

'Find her!' Alice cries, and Tomlin reacts quickly to that

command by leaving her and frantically looking around the promenade before picking a direction and running in it, clearly hoping that he will get lucky and has chosen the right way to go to find the person who has taken the baby. But has he? Like everyone else here, I have no idea. While many people have stopped and some are trying to offer their assistance, it's clear nobody has a clue who might have taken the child and why.

Then I suddenly remember.

The abduction of a child is very serious but it's also unusual. It's not the kind of thing that a person does on a whim, randomly stealing an infant that doesn't belong to them and hoping to get away with it. Something as drastic and devastating as that requires a damaged person, but also a person who has thought about doing something like that before. The act itself might have been spontaneous and opportune but everything leading up to that moment can't have been.

Whoever has taken Alice's child must have desperately wanted a child of their own.

And who do I know who fits that bill?

Victoria.

With the thoughts in my head whirring at a million miles per hour, I think about whether or not it could be possible that she is the one behind the missing child. I already know that she got up off the floor after I pushed her and left her flat. While I don't know where she went after that, she could have been down here. She could have been following me for all I know and, if she was, she would have seen Alice and Tomlin grabbing me, meaning she might also have seen that, in all the madness, they had temporarily left an infant unprotected.

Could it be her? She did try to take Cecilia, so why the hell not. But while I might just have figured out who is behind this, that doesn't mean it's good news, because having seen how deranged Victoria was earlier when she was holding Cecilia in her arms and refusing to give her back to me, I can't say I'm optimistic that this is going to end well for Alice and her child.

But I have to help in any way I can because, despite the crazy history between us, Alice and I share the same bond.

A mother and a child. Nothing is more precious than that.

That's why, instead of worrying about self-preservation, for the first time in a long time, I put someone else's needs in front of my own.

'I think I might know who has her,' I say. Alice stops crying and looks up at me, desperation etched all over her tear-stained face, and I can see that, in this moment, she doesn't care who I am or what I have done to her before.

She only wants me to help her.

So I try.

'I think my neighbour might have her,' I say. 'She tried to take my baby before, so if there's anyone around here who is capable of doing something like this, it's her.'

The man takes hold of my arm again, as if he thinks I'm playing some game and I'm about to escape, but I'm not and I think Alice sees that even if he doesn't.

'Where is she?' Alice asks, the desperation seeping through every pore of her body.

'I don't know but I can help you find her,' I say before looking at the man who is still holding onto my arm, which is a hint that I can only be of assistance if I'm not being restrained so forcefully.

I still don't know who this guy is, and he doesn't seem at all keen to let go of me, but Alice thinks about it for a second before she tells him what to do.

'Ian, let go of her,' she says and at least I now have a name for this person. But Ian doesn't seem keen on doing what he's just been told.

'This could be a ploy. She might run,' he says, but I shake my head.

'No. I want to help you. I swear,' I say, though I know that giving my word might not mean very much to the woman I framed for murder.

'Just help me find my baby,' Alice begs, and that mother-to-mother plea gives me the strength to pull my arm away from Ian and do something about this problem.

With my baby in my arms, I am fully committed to reuniting Alice with hers, and so I begin looking all around the promenade, scanning the sea of faces and looking for any sight of Victoria. I see Tomlin still rushing around, looking into prams and chasing after anybody who has a baby, but he doesn't seem to be making much progress.

Knowing I need to do better, I rush to a bench and stand up on it, giving me a higher vantage point from which to see the crowd. I then look down towards one end of the promenade – down there, everybody is walking at generally the same pace.

But there is one person running.

Fixing my eyes on the woman who is clearly in a rush, I try to figure out if it is Victoria and if she is carrying a baby.

Then she looks back and I see two things.

I see that it is my neighbour.

And I also see that she has Alice's child with her.

THIRTY-ONE

ALICE

I can't believe this is happening. I became so obsessed with catching Fern that I neglected my child and now I might have lost her forever.

While I might have only thought it before, now it seems it is official.

I am the world's worst mother.

However, despite all the nights I wished for somebody else to be able to look after Evelyn and that she could be anybody else's problem but mine, I now want nothing more than to be reunited with her. I took her for granted and didn't appreciate what a blessing she was in my life, far too consumed in my own problems and my need for revenge that I forgot to enjoy her. I feel guilty for that now it's been taken away from me, but will I get the chance to rectify it?

Or have I lost Evelyn forever?

'I can see her! She's down there!' Fern cries from where she stands on a bench, and I leap to my feet and look in the direction she is pointing. I can't see exactly who she is pointing at, nor can I see my baby because there are too many bodies blocking the way. However, Fern tells me that she has my child and says we need to go quickly if we are to catch up to her.

It's crazy but it was only a few moments ago that I hated this woman with every fibre of my being, and was revelling in the fact that I had been the one to catch her and tell her that it was all over. But now I am putting all my trust into her that she can be the one to help me get Evelyn back – if that wasn't crazy enough, Fern actually seems eager to help me.

Far from being the most selfish woman that I have ever known, Fern seems committed to helping me and I'm not going to stand in her way if she can be of assistance. So far, she's offering a lot more than Tomlin or Ian have done.

'This way!' Fern cries as she runs as fast as she can with her child in her arms and, for a second, I fear this might all be some kind of ruse and she could just be fleeing again. Tricking me now when I'm at my most desperate would actually be the cruellest thing she has ever done to me, and that is saying a lot, but it's not the case and I know that because Fern is pointing out the person we are following as we go.

'Can you see her? Over there? In the blue sweater!' Fern cries and, a second later, I do see who she is referring to. I also see that the woman in question is certainly in a rush of her own and, as her body moves, I catch a glimpse of what, or rather who, she is holding, and when I do I recognise the colour of Evelyn's outfit.

She definitely has my baby.

'Stop that woman!' I cry at the top of my lungs, hoping that somebody ahead of us can come to our aid and hold up the abductor before she can do anything even worse than taking a child.

Like panicking and jumping out in front of any of the moving vehicles that are driving beside this promenade.

The thought of Evelyn coming to harm makes me feel sick.

It's only now that I truly appreciate the lengths a parent will go to in order to save their child. I'll literally do anything to get Evelyn back safe and well, but just how far am I going to have to go here? I still don't know, as Fern tells me that Victoria can be stopped, we just need to catch her before she can do anything terrible.

It sounds like Fern is speaking from experience. Things only become more urgent when I see Evelyn being taken from the promenade and carried up the path on a hill that towers over this rugged part of the Cornish coastline.

'Where is she going?' I cry, but the answer to that is sadly an obvious one.

She is going up that hill, and considering how high it is on top and the sheer cliff faces that stand above the sea, I am fearful for what she might be planning to do when she gets up there.

'Somebody stop her! Please!' I cry, but everybody ahead of us seems either too baffled by what is going on to help or too afraid to get involved because the situation must seem too risky for them to put themselves and potentially their own children into.

I get that but it's not helping me – as I keep running I can barely catch my breath. But Fern is right alongside me, running with her baby in tow and, together, we ascend the path that leads up the hill until we make it to the top.

The wind is extremely strong up here and is nosily blowing all around us. But above it, I can make out the sounds of the waves crashing against the rocks far below the cliff. The sound is an ominous one as it proves just how dangerous this situation has become. Things only get worse when I see the woman who has my baby stopping right on the edge of the cliff. She seems to just be staring out to sea, as if her mind is far away from this precarious place right here. But as she hears us getting nearer, she turns to face us.

'Stay back! Don't come any closer,' she cries, her eyes wild and her expression pained.

That threat is enough to make me and Fern stop where we are. As Tomlin and Ian catch up to us, the four of us stare at the woman who holds all the power in this situation.

'Please, just give me my baby back,' I beg, having to shout loudly so my voice is heard above the wind and the waves below us. That desperate plea seems to have no impact on the woman who is holding precious Evelyn so close to that sheer drop. My stomach churns as turbulently as the sea beneath my baby's little kicking legs. And despite praying for the best outcome, I get the horrible feeling that this can only possibly end in disaster.

That is until Fern has a suggestion.

THIRTY-TWO

FERN

'Let me talk to her,' I say to Alice, my voice only loud enough for her to hear. 'I know her. She was a friend once. I can get her to stop this before it gets any worse.'

She looks at me and can tell that I am serious, but what I am asking means that she has to put all her trust into the woman who has caused so much pain in her life already. What if she agrees and I fail? Then she would have to live with the knowledge that not only did I hurt her again, but that she put her little girl's life in the hands of a dangerous and deadly killer who would never have offered to help her if she hadn't just caught me unexpectedly. But I am telling the truth; Victoria was a friend of mine once, so maybe I am the best-placed person here to try and talk her down. I was obviously correct when I said I knew who might have taken Evelyn and, if it wasn't for me, Alice never would have spotted the abductor on the packed promenade. Despite our chequered past, I haven't let her down so far today.

I don't know what else to do but what I do know is that every time Alice tries to get closer to the crazy woman on the edge of the cliff, Victoria takes another step closer to the edge, so she can't keep trying to stop this herself.

Tomlin has a go at resolving this situation suddenly, employing some of the skills he has learnt in the police force in dealing with dangerous people, but that does no good either and he is forced to stop when he also realises that getting closer is only making things worse as well.

It seems like we don't have many options, which is why I ask Alice again for the green light to try and stop this myself.

'Please. Just get her back,' she says to me, all her trust transferred to me in this moment. But it's not all one way because then I do something that shows that I trust her too.

I hand Cecilia to her.

As she takes my daughter, she looks down at her face and possibly wonders what kind of life my little girl has already had with her mother being on the run. I'm sure she can imagine that it must have been hard.

'I'll do everything I can,' I assure Alice before I step towards Victoria, who quickly puts a hand up to signal to me to stay where I am.

'Get away from me!' she cries as the wind swirls and Evelyn continues to dangle over the edge. I'm aware that if I can't get through to this woman then there is a very big chance this ends in disaster, for both Alice and I. She might lose her daughter, while mine will be taken away as I'm arrested, and then neither of us will have anything.

Nobody will have won.

Everything will have been lost.

That cannot happen.

'Victoria, it's okay. I just want to talk to you,' I say. 'I'm your friend.'

'No, you're not! You attacked me!' she cries, which I obviously did, so that doesn't really help my cause.

'I'm sorry about that, but you know why I had to do it. You

were trying to take my baby and that's not a nice thing to do. A child belongs with their mother. That child there belongs with hers. She's here now, you can see her. Look how upset she is.'

I gesture to Alice behind me and the distraught woman holding Cecilia has tears running down her cheeks.

'Give her back to her mum,' I say calmly. 'It's the right thing to do. You don't want to hurt her. I know you're not a bad person. We can talk about this. Get you some help. This doesn't have to get any worse.'

'You have no idea what it's like!' Victoria suddenly screams at me. 'Seeing everyone else with a baby when I can't have one! It's not fair!'

'But it's not fair to hurt her, is it?' I say, pointing at the child in her arms. 'She's totally innocent and look how upset she is. Just let her go.'

'No, it's too late. I've already made too many mistakes. There's nothing else I can do. What have I got to lose? I'm not going to prison and I'm not going back to that flat! I hate it!'

'I hated it too,' I admit. 'But it wasn't so bad, was it? We had each other. I used to love our chats. Watching you play with Cecilia. Sharing a cup of tea with you. It was nice, wasn't it?'

Victoria looks like she is relaxing a little, so I carry on.

'I know exactly what it is like to make mistakes. To do things that you shouldn't do, things that are out of character and end up hurting other people. I know all about that and I know how much it hurts to feel like you have lost control. But it's never too late to change and do the right thing. It's never too late to apologise.'

Victoria seems to be really listening to me now, so I keep going but, as I speak, I'm aware that I'm not just talking to her anymore but to Alice and Tomlin behind me.

'I have plenty of regrets,' I admit. 'I wish I hadn't done so many of the things that I've done and look what my life has become because of it. But you still have a chance. You have time to stop before you make it worse. Please, believe me when I tell you that you do not want to make things worse for yourself.'

Now I have tears in my eyes as I carry on. 'My husband hurt me, but I never should have hurt him,' I say, loudly and clearly as if not just talking to those around me but to Drew in the afterlife too. 'I was a good person. I am a good person. I just made mistakes and I can't take them back. I regret what I did to him, just like I regret what I did to Rory and Greg and to her!'

I turn and point at Alice.

'I'm so sorry, Alice. I'm sorry for what I put you through. And I'm sorry for you being here now and having to go through this. You don't deserve this.'

Turning back to Victoria, I take a step nearer as I keep talking.

'It's too late for me. No matter what I do next, I'm always going to be remembered as the Black Widow. The woman who plotted to kill her cheating husband. The person who framed an innocent woman for murder. The woman who killed to keep her secrets safe and who ran away when things got tough. That's me, that's my life story and I can't change that. But you can change your story. You don't want to be remembered as the woman who killed an innocent child. That's not you. You are warm and friendly and funny and kind and you can still have a good life, it's not too late. I promise you, Victoria, it's not too late.'

I'm closer to her now and Victoria isn't moving back, which is good because there isn't much of the clifftop left behind her to move back on to.

With my hands out in front of me, I smile at Victoria and tell her that everything is okay.

'Just hand her to me,' I say calmly.

Victoria still looks unsure, but she isn't telling me to stop approaching her and, as I reach her, I make sure to focus on her face rather than on the big drop just behind her.

In that moment, the wind drops, and everything goes quiet.

'It's okay,' I say. 'Trust me, you won't regret doing the right thing.'

Maybe Victoria can see how much regret I have for doing the wrong thing, but she listens to me and hands the baby over.

Looking down at the child in my arms, I instantly see parts of Drew in her. She has his eyes, those piercing blue irises that dazzled me when I first met him, and, for a second, it's impossible not to see his whole face before me. It should have been me who had his baby, not anybody else, but given all the crazy things that have happened, perhaps me holding his mistress's child is not the strangest thing that has occurred since his affair began.

Once it becomes clear that the danger is over, I hear Alice let out a huge cry of 'thank you' behind us. I'm not sure if it's for me or for Victoria, but as we move away from the cliff edge, it doesn't really matter because it's over now.

Or is it?

As I return Alice's baby to her, I have no idea what is going to happen next.

Judging by the look on her face, neither does she.

THIRTY-THREE

ALICE

I remember when I used to hate looking into this face.

But not anymore.

As I lean down over the crib and pick my baby up, I am no longer consumed by feelings of regret, frustration and anxiety, nor do I feel overwhelmed at the size of the task that being a mother entails. Now I just feel happiness that my daughter is safe and well and, as Evelyn snuggles in my arms, I give her a kiss on the head and tell her that everything is going to be alright.

For the first time in a long time, that might actually be the truth.

It's been two months since I caught Fern in Cornwall, though it hadn't quite gone how I imagined it would. The pleasure and satisfaction I felt as I grabbed hold of her and told her that her time on the run was over was quickly overtaken by a desperate desire to be reunited with Evelyn, after she had been taken by a distressed and dangerous woman.

I'll never quite know why Fern chose to help me that day rather than revert to her old ways and only look out for herself, but she did and, for that, I will be forever grateful. She could have tried to get away while I was on my knees on that promenade, wailing at the heavens, and I would have been powerless to stop her because, in that moment, all I cared about was that my child had been taken. She could have disappeared with her own baby, and I assume that if that had happened and she had vanished again, I would not have had the energy to ever try and find her one more time. But as it was, she came to my aid and was able to talk Victoria down from that clifftop, saving Evelyn and myself, for that matter, in the process.

So what happened next?

That was actually the question Fern asked me not long after we handed our children back to each other. As we had stood there on top of that windswept cliff with our babies in our arms, the concept of revenge and justice seemed wrong. What seemed right was that we were two women who had been put on a collision course thanks to things that we had little control over.

Fern had not asked for her husband to have an affair with me, and I hadn't asked him to follow me to Arberness after I had ended the affair. Both those things had happened, but they had been driven by Drew, the doctor who always seemed to get his own way and to hell with anyone else. Although neither of us could completely say we were victims after everything that had gone on, we were bonded by the sad fact that our lives had been much easier before the doctor messed with them.

That was why, instead of telling Tomlin to arrest Fern or call for backup, I told him that I wanted some time alone with the doctor's wife so that we could speak openly about all that had occurred.

Tomlin had not seemed keen on that idea at first, although, like me, his hatred of Fern had been lessened somewhat because he had just witnessed her save a child's life, so he agreed. But rather than stand around like a spare part, he took Fern's suggestion that he should offer assistance to Victoria, the mentally ill woman who was clearly in desperate need of assistance, and he did just that, walking away with her and telling her that rather than be in trouble, she was going to get the help she needed now.

Fern and I also walked down off that clifftop, a child in each of our arms, and we didn't stop walking until we had entered a cafe and ordered ourselves strong cups of coffee. Then, it was there where we discussed our next move.

Evelyn is due for a feed so I'm carrying her downstairs as I think back to that coffee with Fern and that unexpectedly calm conversation that occurred over 500 miles away from where I am now. While I am back in the peaceful tranquillity of Arberness, it was at a table in a cafe in Cornwall where I can honestly say that I finally was able to move on with my life instead of continuing to live in the past.

As we were served our coffee and as our two children stared at each other's faces and were mesmerised by the sight of another young person, like many children are when they're around each other, Fern and I opened up about everything that had happened and the impact it had had on the pair of us.

Going first, I told Fern what I felt was the truth.

'I was wrong to start that affair with your husband,' I had said, swallowing hard just before I spoke. 'There's no denying that. But I tried to do the right thing when I decided to move away with Rory. I left Manchester to get away from Drew and, as far as I was concerned, the affair was over. I had no idea that he would follow me to Arberness and I regret that he did, just like I regret that I allowed our affair to restart.'

Fern had respectfully listened to my side of the story as I'd gone on.

'I know it was wrong and we did deserve for the affair to be exposed and for our marriages to be ruined, but the worst that should have happened was a divorce,' I'd explained. 'I did not deserve to go to prison for a crime I didn't commit.'

Surprisingly, Fern had agreed with me before giving her version of events.

'I was so consumed with a need for revenge back then,' she had admitted. 'It took me over so much that I didn't take a step back and see things from anybody else's point of view. It's only recently I have realised the kind of hold my late husband had over other people.'

'I've read emails from Drew that clearly show me that he was the instigator of the affair and kept it going even when you voiced your concerns,' Fern had gone on, showing sympathy towards me, which I appreciated. 'I also accept that I went way too far in my quest for revenge and should never have enlisted Rory to help me kill Drew, nor should I have hurt Rory to keep him quiet. Neither of them deserved to lose their life and you certainly didn't deserve to go to prison.'

As we had both clearly demonstrated a willingness to be open and honest, I had gone on then to give Fern a little insight into what prison life had been like for me.

'I wouldn't wish a place like that on my worst enemy,' I had said, well aware that it had only been mere minutes before that conversation when Fern had been such an enemy to me. 'I was brutally attacked in prison and, while I didn't know it at the time, I was carrying a child then and could easily have lost her.'

Fern had looked genuinely horrified at that and apologised again, though after I'd seen how sorry she was, I did remind her that my affair had started it all and apologised myself. Fern had then gone on to give me an insight into her life since she had been on the run and, as she did, it seemed as grim as what I went through in prison.

'Just because I was technically free, it didn't mean that I had gotten away with anything,' Fern had said. 'I've spent every day looking over my shoulder, wondering if my time was up and I was going to be arrested. I've lived in squalor, before I had Cecilia and after, and I've laid awake night after night worrying about what would happen to my baby if I had to spend the rest of my life behind bars.'

It must have been the presence of those two children, their little eyes bright and their bodies all wriggly on our laps, that was the main reason behind the two of us mellowing greatly about what had happened. For some reason, introducing a couple of kids into our toxic relationship certainly helped ease some of the tensions because, despite everything that had happened, we realised that we no longer just had that charming doctor in common anymore.

We also shared the fact that we were simply two mothers who wanted the best for their child.

That fact made me realise that the best thing for Cecilia, Fern's pretty girl, was not to have her mother go to prison for the rest of her life. Calling the police seemed to be the wrong course of action, especially after the selfless and brave act she had just completed on top of the cliff that loomed large on the other side of the cafe window. That's why I decided there and then that I was not going to see out my need for revenge all the way to its grisly conclusion. How could I watch Fern being taken away in handcuffs and her baby handed off to a social worker, when I would go home with my baby and be reminded of what Fern had done to save her every time I looked in her face? But it wasn't just about me, it was about Fern too. Despite her not having yet spent a minute in police custody for any of the things she had done, I could clearly see that she had been punished, nonetheless.

It's true what they say about people who get away with something they shouldn't. They spend the rest of their life sleeping with one eye open. I knew that was Fern's fate even if I let her walk out of that cafe to get on with her life, which is why, in the end, that is exactly what I told her I was willing to do.

'It's over. Let's just walk away and try and get on with the rest of our lives,' I had said to Fern, showing an inner strength to not need revenge that I only wish the doctor's wife had possessed back when this all started.

'How can you be so forgiving?' Fern had asked me then. 'You ruined my marriage but I ruined your life.'

'Because you just saved my child,' I had explained. 'That shows me you're not an evil person. You've just made mistakes. Big mistakes, terrible mistakes, but you're not totally past the point of redemption. You saved my baby, and you have one of your own to look after. If it wasn't for those two things then I'd gladly see you arrested, but now I can't. So just accept this and leave. Go back on the run and try and find some peace with your child. I will go home and try to do the same with mine.'

'Thank you,' Fern had said then, before asking one very poignant question. 'Do you think we can find some peace?'

'I hope so,' is all I had been able to say to that and, with that comment, our bitter relationship was over.

As always with us two, things had never been quite as they seemed. Fern had always imagined me as some cruel, cold-hearted homewrecker and I had seen her as some vengeful force who didn't give a damn about anyone but herself, but we both realised that day that such assumptions were no longer true. Which was why we felt like we could both walk away from each other for good.

And that's exactly what we did.

As I prepare a bottle for Evelyn in my kitchen, I wonder what Fern is doing now. Probably preparing a meal for her baby too. That tends to be how the days go for parents in our position. But while I can guess as to what she is doing, I have absolutely no clue as to where she might be doing it. That's because after we had both vowed to leave the other one alone, I took Evelyn and left that cafe, and I haven't seen Fern or Cecilia since.

Walking away from the woman I had spent so long chasing felt surprisingly triumphant, like I was communicating to the universe that I was finally willing to let the past go and move on with my life. I proved that was the case when, after linking back up with Tomlin, I told him that upon returning to Arberness I wished for our relationship to come to an end.

He knew why, his brief fling with Siobhan had sealed his fate, but that didn't stop him trying to convince me how he loved me.

'We can make it work,' he had tried, clearly not ready to lose me, but my mind had already been made up. 'I'll never do anything like that ever again.'

'I said the same thing to myself when I ended things with Drew the first time,' I had replied, speaking from grim experience. 'Yet I ended up doing it again, so I know just saying words are meaningless.'

Tomlin had struggled to argue with that, no doubt seeing that my mind was made up, but I added my extra reason for things ending between us.

'It's not just what you did behind my back. It's everything, Your job. Your connection to Fern, to Drew, to my past. I need a clean break from all of it. It's the only way I can move on and be the best mum I can be to Evelyn. I hope you can understand that.'

Tomlin had looked upset but accepting then, and he did understand, aware that his connection to the past had probably always meant our relationship was ultimately doomed and the liaison with Siobhan was just the final nail in the coffin.

As for Siobhan, perhaps unsurprisingly, she hasn't been in touch with me since I left her stranded by the side of the motorway. While I have no idea what has happened to her, I don't really care because I don't need friends like her anymore.

Before we parted, Tomlin had something he wanted to know, something he was struggling to get his head around.

'How could you let Fern go when you had her?' he had asked me. 'You spent so long wanting revenge and then, when you could have had it, you allowed her to walk away and stay free?'

'She saved Evelyn,' I had replied. 'That's far more valuable to me than some need for revenge. I have a child to love for the rest of my life. That's all I care about now and that's all I will focus on.'

Tomlin then understood why I had done that, having witnessed the drama on the clifftop for himself. Possibly proving how he was also willing to become more selfless, he accepted that he could go back to work and continue being the detective who let her get away rather than keep trying in vain for some shot at professional redemption.

After driving back to Arberness, the two of us said our good-byes and he left for Carlisle while I closed the front door to my home and contemplated that it was now just me and my little girl.

But unlike before, I was not worried about that.

I was happy.

I am happy now as I start feeding Evelyn and see her eyes light up as she stares up at me. I can confidently say that I am the happiest I have been in a long time.

As for Fern?

Who knows.

It's time for me to forget about her.

Maybe I'll read about her on the news one day. She could still get found by the police because I know they are always looking.

But then again, maybe not.

Something tells me that a resourceful woman like her will find a way to keep evading them.

Something tells me that the doctor's wife will be doing just fine.

EPILOGUE

FIVE YEARS LATER

There's a real beauty about living in a village. Being able to walk everywhere. Knowing all the locals by their first name. Not having to worry about serious crime.

I like that last one the most.

Yes, it's official. After spending so long as a city-lover, I am now completely converted, and I love village life. Arberness is where it started for me and, as I walk along these quiet streets and smile at the friendly butcher who offers me a greeting before quickly mentioning a sale he is currently offering, it's almost as if I am in Arberness now.

Almost.

While this scenic and tranquil place I am currently walking through does have a lot of similarities with that small section of the map in Northern England, I am many miles away from there. I'm actually in an entirely different country altogether. As I pause briefly at the butcher's, and make a polite check on the discounted prices that are being offered as part of the sale, I get another reminder of that. That's because the numbers on the price tags beside all the fresh meats are accompanied by the local currency here, and instead of it being a pound sign, it is a Euro.

That's because I'm living in France.

Using some of the language I have learnt since I have been here, I thank the butcher in French for alerting me to this sale before politely telling him that I am okay for the time being, but will be back this weekend to buy some sausages from him. I'm not the only person who has something to say in French. That's because, after looking down at my daughter beside me, she offers a few words in her new language herself before we are back on our way, headed in the direction of her school.

I giggle to myself a little as I go because, as somebody who never thought they would be clever enough to speak anything other than English, I am actually doing a pretty good job of conversing in a new tongue. It turns out that learning a new language is less about being clever and more about time and commitment. Isn't that the same for most things? I've certainly put a lot of effort into being able to speak French and it has only helped me fit into my new home even more.

It's important to fit in anywhere, of course.

But especially because I'm a criminal hiding from the police overseas.

Cecilia asks me what is funny, but I just say it's nothing before commenting on how pretty she looks with the pink bow that I tied into her blonde hair this morning. She requested it and I figured it would be acceptable at school, so I obliged and now she is very proud of her new look that she gets to show off to all her classmates today. I'm proud too, but not just because she has a pink bow in her hair. It's because she is growing into a funny, polite and clever girl, despite all the upheaval she has already endured in her young life.

If I was worried about what the impact of a life on the run would have on me, I've been even more worried about what the consequences of it would be on my daughter. But I guess it's true what they say about little ones. They are resilient, though I do think that I'm pretty resilient myself.

All these years later and I'm still going strong.

As I walk on through the village, I am well aware that I have put considerable distance between myself and the places where I committed my serious crimes. I am also aware there is nowhere I can go on this planet that will allow me to escape the punishment for them if I was to ever be caught and taken back to England. That's why I have to be constantly careful, and it's why being able to speak the same language of the locals here only helps me integrate myself into my new community even more, reducing the chances that one of them figures out who I really am. But while the story of the Black Widow was big news in the UK, nobody in France seems to know much about it. My face certainly isn't on the front covers of any of the newspapers here, nor is it flashing up on any TV screens during news bulletins, and that's just fine by me. It's been five years now since I last saw anybody who really knows who I am and what I have done and so far, so good.

That person was Alice.

She is the only reason I am free today.

While I was not selfishly trying to help myself when I stood on that clifftop and negotiated with Victoria, only trying to save a child's life because I really was the best-placed person to do that, there is no denying that my actions that day helped Alice forgive me. If Victoria hadn't taken her daughter then Alice would have very happily had me arrested, and both me and Cecilia would have a very different life to the one we have now. There would be no peaceful existence in this quiet part of France, where locals and expats mix freely while welcoming a few tourists every summer to sample the local vineyards and soak up some of the sun.

Alice will never be able to forget what I did to her, but she did forgive, and I can say the same about her and Drew. Their affair started all of this and now, years later, things can never be the same as they once were. All that matters is that the two of us get on with the rest of our lives as best we can, making the most of the opportunities that the next few decades give to us, and that's an opportunity the late doctor we shared does not have.

As the gates to Cecilia's school come into view, I feel her tighten her grip on my right hand and know she is a little anxious, as she always is when it becomes time for us to part. Having been inseparable since she was born, barring that one frightful event when Victoria tried to take her away from me, it's understandable that my daughter has a little separation anxiety. I have it too, but we're working on it. While it's still early days in terms of Cecilia's school life, she understands that her mummy will always be waiting for her at the end of the day when classes are over.

'Have a good day,' I tell my daughter before I kneel down and give her a kiss on the cheek.

She still looks a little unsure about leaving me, as she has done for the past three weeks since her first school year started, but she has made a few friends. When she sees one of them up ahead, she looks less apprehensive and more playful.

'Bye, Mummy,' she says to me before she hurries to join her friend, and then I watch as the two youngsters enter the school, ready for a busy day of learning ahead.

But they're not the only ones who are hoping to learn something today, because after checking the time, I rush off for my own engagement, albeit one that I hope will be slightly more interesting than learning maths or geography. That's because I'm going to go and find out if I really am ready for something that I have ignored ever since I killed Greg in that hotel room in Manchester on my fortieth birthday.

I am going to see if I am ready to start dating again.

I can't quite decide if the butterflies I feel fluttering in my

stomach are a good sign or a bad one, as I make my way to the
meeting place for my date. It might help that I'm a little nervous
because it shows that I care, but then again, it might be a sign
that I am really not ready for this and should just go back to my
flat and tidy up before Cecilia is home again, making another
mess of the place. I have to try, because not only do I not want
to spend the rest of my life sleeping alone in bed, but I promised
the man who asked me out on a date that I would meet him, so
it would be rude of me not to go.

The man in question is called Pierre and he is a regular
customer at the bakery I work at four mornings a week. The
bakery, a cute little place that serves bread, scones and cakes
that all look and smell absolutely delicious, is the place I have
been working at since I was fortunate enough to be given a
chance serving customers on the front desk. While I'm not
skilled enough to bake the bread or create the cakes yet, I am
capable of handing packages of pastries to paying customers and
putting their money in the till. I am very grateful for the chance
to earn some money here. It's not a particularly high-paying job
but it doesn't have to be because my cost of living isn't high
here. It is a sociable job though – by working at the bakery, I
have got to know everybody in the village, and it has really
made me feel a part of this place. I also like the fact that as an
employee of the bakery, I'm entitled to take home any leftovers
that haven't sold that day, and free food is always helpful,
though it hasn't done my waistline much good, I have to admit.

But what's the point of living in France if you can't
overindulge on croissants and pains au chocolat?

As I pass the bakery and offer a wave to my colleagues who
are on shift today, I think about how I'd always been hoping that
the handsome customer who came in every Tuesday and Friday
morning might one day ask me out on a date.

And then it happened.

Pierre, having always ordered a coffee and a croissant ever

since I had known him, asked for something else last Friday morning as I served him. He asked me if I would like to get breakfast with him at the cafe that overlooks the village square. I'd been shocked that he, a dashing Frenchman always dressed impeccably, was interested in me, a foreigner dressed in white overalls and smelling of pastry. But I had said yes before he had chance to change his mind and now the date is almost upon us.

The cafe comes into view as I cross the cobbled square and, as the church bell chimes nine times in the tower that looms above me, I know that Cecilia will be starting her first class of the day now. I also know that I'm slightly late because I should be sat at the table with Pierre already, so I hurry and, when I enter the cafe, I see him sitting at a table by the window, perusing the menu.

He flashes me a warm smile when he sees me entering before getting up out of his seat and greeting me like a true gentleman, so he's already off to a good start. I make sure to make a good impression too, complimenting him on his smart jacket before saying that I love this cafe, which is a subtle hint that he did well in choosing this place for our first date.

The two of us make small talk in English, thankfully, while we decide what to order, and once the waitress has been to our table to note our requests, we are both ready to move the conversation onto slightly more interesting topics than the weather and how many people are passing through the square on this sunny morning.

Pierre is interested in origins, more specifically my time in England and how I ended up here, and while this could have been a very tricky subject, I made sure to prepare for it meticulously last night as I was lying in bed and visualising what I would say. That's why I'm able to calmly and convincingly tell him that I moved to France after falling in love with this country while on holiday here. After the untimely and unfortunate death of Cecilia's father, this village seemed like a great place for the two of us to make a fresh start.

Pierre is quick to offer his sympathies regarding the passing of my daughter's dad and I thank him while aware that, with this sounding like a sensitive subject, he is unlikely to pry much further into it, especially on a first date. Then I neatly steer the conversation back onto him, asking him how he ended up living here rather than in a more populated place, like Paris, which is only forty miles away.

'Like you, I needed a change of scene,' Pierre tells me as the scent of coffee and eggs fills my nostrils in this cute eatery. 'My job could be a demanding one in a city but here, it's much more forgiving. But we're not at work now, so I'm happy to talk about something else.'

'I see,' I reply as the waitress brings us our coffees. After she sets them down, I am far too curious to just leave this topic there, so I smile at Pierre before asking him, 'What is it you do for work?'

Pierre thanks the waitress before looking up at me to answer my question. When he does, I can scarcely believe it.

'I'm a doctor,' he says calmly. 'So nothing that exciting ever happens to me.'

I stare at the man sitting opposite me and think about the million and one ways I could reply to that statement of his. In the end, I just decide to simply smile and agree with him.

'Yeah,' I say with a nod of my head. 'I hear that being a doctor can be pretty boring.'

A LETTER FROM DANIEL

Dear reader,

I want to say a huge thank you for choosing to read *The Doctor's Mistress*. I hope you enjoyed following the misadventures of Fern Devlin for a third time! If you did enjoy it and would like to keep up to date with all my latest Bookouture releases and read my free short story, *The Killer Wife*, please sign up to my Bookouture newsletter at the following link. Your email address will never be shared and you can unsubscribe at any time.

www.bookouture.com/daniel-hurst

I hope you loved this third book in *The Doctor's Wife* series and if you did, I would be very grateful if you could write an honest review. I'd like to hear what you think!

I also enjoy hearing from my readers, and you can get in touch with me directly at my email address daniel@danielhurst books.com. I reply to every message! You can also visit my website where you can download a free psychological thriller called *Just One Second* and join my personal weekly newsletter, where you can hear all about my future writing as well as my adventures with my wife, Harriet, and daughter, Penny!

Thank you,

Daniel

KEEP IN TOUCH WITH DANIEL

www.danielhurstbooks.com

facebook.com/danielhurstbooks
instagram.com/danielhurstbooks

PUBLISHING TEAM

Turning a manuscript into a book requires the efforts of many people. The publishing team at Bookouture would like to acknowledge everyone who contributed to this publication.

Audio
Alba Proko
Sinead O'Connor
Melissa Tran

Commercial
Lauren Morrissette
Jil Thielen
Imogen Allport

Data and analysis
Mark Alder
Mohamed Bussuri

Editorial
Natasha Harding
Lizzie Brien

Copyeditor
Laura Gerrard

Made in the USA
Middletown, DE
08 September 2024

60632769R00138